"According To You, Bradley Is My Son. Which Means I Might As Well Start Learning The Ropes Now."

Dark eyes flashing, he stalked toward her, closing the distance between them and making her shrink back.

"And I thought you could teach me what I need to know," he whispered, his gaze locked on her lips. "In the evenings, when you're not busy."

"All right," she agreed, almost as though someone else were speaking for her.

"I'm going to kiss you now, Haylie Smith," he murmured in a low, mesmerizing voice.

"Why?"

He grinned. "Because I've been thinking about it all night. I want to feel your lips, know what you taste like."

She knew she should say no, push him away, but darned if her body would listen to reason.

Dear Reader,

I can't tell you how excited I am to be bringing
Dynasties: The Jarrods to a close. It is always a thrill to
be involved in such a wonderful series and to get to work
with so many other great authors.

But even more special for me is the fact that
Inheriting His Secret Christmas Baby marks my return
to the Silhouette Desire line after a short hiatus, and
Trevor and Haylie's story was right up my alley. It has
everything I love—a secret baby, a touch of blackmail
and lots of wonderful, sexy romance, all set in the
beautiful snow-covered mountains of Aspen, Colorado.

I hope you enjoy!

Heidi Betts

www.HeidiBetts.com

HEIDI BETTS

INHERITING HIS SECRET CHRISTMAS BABY

Published by Silhouette Books
America's Publisher of Contemporary Romance

*For Diana Ventimiglia. We got to work together only briefly once,
then briefly once again, but I cannot thank you enough for all of your help
and wonderful support. I hope our paths cross again in the future and that the third time
for us is the charm. Wishing you the very best always! (And thanks for giving me a story
in this continuity that I could love from the very beginning.)*

Special thanks and acknowledgment to Heidi Betts for her contribution
to the Dynasties: The Jarrods miniseries.

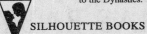

SILHOUETTE BOOKS

®

PLEASE RECYCLE

THIS PRODUCT IS RECYCLABLE

Recycling programs
for this product may
not exist in your area.

ISBN-13: 978-0-373-73068-1

INHERITING HIS SECRET CHRISTMAS BABY

Copyright © 2010 by Harlequin Books S.A.

Visit Silhouette Books at www.eHarlequin.com

Printed in U.S.A.

Books by Heidi Betts

Silhouette Desire

Bought by a Millionaire #1638
Blame it on the Blackout #1662
When the Lights Go Down #1686
Seven-Year Seduction #1709
Mr. and Mistress #1723
Bedded Then *Wed* #1761
Blackmailed into Bed #1779
Fortune's Forbidden Woman #1801
Christmas in His Royal Bed #1833
Inheriting His Secret Christmas Baby #2055

HEIDI BETTS

An avid romance reader since junior high school, Heidi knew early on that she wanted to write these wonderful stories of love and adventure. It wasn't until her freshman year of college, however, when she spent the entire night reading a romance novel instead of studying for finals, that she decided to take the road less traveled and follow her dream. In addition to reading and writing romance, she is the founder of her local Romance Writers of America chapter and has a tendency to take injured and homeless animals of every species into her Central Pennsylvania home.

Heidi loves to hear from readers. You can write to her at P.O. Box 99, Kylertown, PA 16847 (a SASE is appreciated but not necessary), or email heidi@heidibetts.com. And be sure to visit www.heidibetts.com for news and information about upcoming books.

From the Last Will and Testament of Don Jarrod

...and to my youngest son, **Trevor,** I leave your mother's wedding band. It's unfortunate that you knew your mother for so short a time. I wish you had been given the opportunity to share more experiences with the woman who loved you more than life itself. You may not have been aware, but the wedding ring she was buried with was not her original ring. This simple white-gold band was all she wanted when we married. Only years later was I able to convince her to accept a more elaborate one. But she never got rid of her ring, and I think she would very much have wanted you, her precious baby boy, to keep and cherish it until you find the right woman to wear it. I hope that day comes soon for you, son.

One

Entering the expansive Jarrod Ridge Manor hotel through a private side entrance, Trevor Jarrod stomped the snow from his heavy ski boots and headed down the long hallway toward his office.

Thick oriental rugs lined the golden, highly glossed wooden floors as he passed his brothers' offices. Some of the doors were closed, others were open, voices and sounds of keyboards or ringing phones drifting out.

Opposite the row of office suites, tall, narrow tables dotted the fog-colored walls, each boasting a cobalt-blue vase that in summer would be stuffed with fresh roses and hydrangeas or other seasonal arrangements. Currently, however, they overflowed with bright red, burgeoning poinsettias to mark the upcoming Christmas holiday.

Stone and wood accents filled this wing of the Manor as well as the rest of the main hotel, which had been the original structure at Jarrod Ridge Resort more than a hundred years before. Since then, the resort had grown by leaps and bounds, with additions to the Manor, and separate lodges, shops and other accommodations being built on and around until the place looked for all the world like a quaint, isolated little village.

But the family's offices were still located here in the main building, and their private living quarters—for those who chose to stay there—still occupied the top floor of the Manor, keeping the Jarrods very tight-knit and in near constant contact, whether they liked it or not.

Reaching his own office, Trevor greeted Diana, personal assistant extraordinaire, before stashing his skis in the wide hidden closet behind her desk.

"How were the slopes this morning?" she asked, tipping her head to one side so that her long, black, curly hair fell over her shoulder.

"Could have been better," he replied, stripping out of his navy-blue ski clothes and switching to a pair of worn Timberlands to go with his jeans and tan cable-knit cashmere sweater.

Casual for office attire, sure, but then so was going to work straight from a run down the slopes. And this was, after all, a ski resort—as well as a spa, summer retreat and host location for one of Colorado's biggest events, the annual Food and Wine Gala. So it paid to have guests see the owners and employees enjoying all the activities and amenities Jarrod Ridge had to offer right along with them.

"I think I'm losing my mojo," he grumbled.

"Nah, you just haven't had as much time as usual to play...I mean, practice," she corrected with a wink.

Wasn't that the truth. In the five months since his

father had passed away, Trevor had been juggling two nearly full-time jobs. Donald Jarrod's will had forced all six of his children to return to Jarrod Ridge to manage the resort or risk losing their shares in the family dynasty.

But as much as he may have been forced to take over as president of marketing for Jarrod Ridge, it certainly hadn't been a hardship for him. After running his own very successful marketing firm in downtown Aspen, the job here came almost as naturally to him as breathing.

Unfortunately, it didn't leave him a lot of time for what he loved most—the outdoors and all the sporting activities it had to offer. In the summer, he spent nearly every minute of his free time hiking, climbing, kayaking or riding his mountain bike. In the winter, he loved to hit the slopes, usually on his skis, but occasionally snowboarding.

Nature was great, and he appreciated it as much as the next person, but for him, it was all about the adventure. The rush. There was nothing in the world like speeding down a snow-slick mountainside, dodging rocks and trees, feeling the cold sting of the wind on his face. Or jumping from a plane at thirteen thousand feet with nothing but a parachute and his own skills to break his fall.

Oh, yeah. He had to get on the ball and figure out what he was going to do about balancing his two vital positions, so he could get back to putting in *normal* workaholic hours and carve out a bit more time on the slopes. But until he found someone he trusted and could truly rely on to take over Jarrod Promotion and Marketing, he was just going to have to deal with it, he supposed.

"Any messages?" he asked Diana, running his

fingers through his dark hair to brush away any excess moisture.

Getting to her feet, she handed him a stack of pink papers. More than he was in the mood to deal with at the moment.

"Before you go into your office..." she began, only to let her words drift off, her bottom lip disappearing between her teeth as she worried it nervously.

"Yes?"

She took a breath and met his gaze. "There's a young woman waiting for you. She's been calling, and insisted on seeing you in person. I started to turn her away, but didn't have the heart, and...well, I just thought she was someone you should deal with personally."

He frowned. Diana might be pixie-petite, but he'd seen her in protective, full linebacker mode. The woman waiting in his office must indeed be brave to have gotten past Diana. Brave, or very convincing.

"Who is she?" he asked. "A company rep wanting us to use their products to supply the Ridge, or a possible client who hasn't been able to catch me at JPM?"

Diana shrugged. "You'll have to ask her yourself. She didn't say, she was just...very determined."

With a sigh, Trevor folded the stack of messages and stuffed them in his pants pocket. "Fine. I'll take care of it."

Pulling open both of the heavy oak doors that separated his office from the reception area, he paused to take in the sweep of his office. The thick Gulistan carpeting. The unlit fireplace built of smooth river stones lining the back wall. And in the center of the room, his heavy, ornately carved desk with its lamp at one corner, computer monitor at the other and stacks of paper at the center.

But no woman in either of the guest chairs waiting to see him.

Closing the doors behind him with a click, he stepped farther inside. As the sound echoed through the room, his espresso-dark leather desk chair tipped slightly before swiveling around to reveal a lovely woman with honey-blond hair and blue eyes. On her lap, leaning back against her chest, was an infant busily chewing on his own hand.

Trevor frowned. Well. The woman was no surprise; Diana had warned him one was waiting to see him. His so-called assistant had failed to mention, however, that said woman had a child with her.

What kind of woman came to a business meeting with a baby in tow? he wondered. Even an impromptu meeting that—judging by the way this one was starting—might not last long.

"My secretary said you needed to speak with me," he said, rounding the desk with every intention of taking her place and relegating her to one of the guest chairs.

If he'd expected her to hop up and bashfully bustle around to the other side of the desk, though, he was doomed to disappointment. She held her ground, remaining seated in *his* executive chair—the one he had special-ordered and waited nearly a month for it to arrive, the one that had taken another month to break in and now cushioned his body like a glove during each of the many long hours he put in here at Jarrod Manor—while she bounced the child up and down on her knees.

"I'm Trevor Jarrod," he offered when she didn't seem eager to fill the chilly silence.

"I know who you are. I've been trying to reach you for the past two months."

Her tone was flat with a trace of annoyance threading through, but also light and extremely feminine. Lifting a hand, she swept a chunk of her straight blond hair behind one ear, revealing a single ruby-red stud that matched the knit V-neck sweater she was wearing with a pair of sleek black slacks.

The baby on her lap was dressed in blue denim overalls with an embroidered train engine on the front pocket and a shirt underneath with dozens more trains covering the white cotton. A boy, Trevor assumed, otherwise he would be looking at a little denim jumper covered in pink butterflies or some such.

As though he sensed Trevor's perusal, the baby gave a smiling gurgle and kicked his legs out in front of him.

Dragging his attention back to the woman who'd fought so hard to gain an audience with him but suddenly seemed at a loss for words, Trevor crossed his arms over his chest and lifted a brow. "And you are…?"

That brought her to her feet, shifting the child in her arms until he was perched on one hip.

How did women do that? Were they born knowing how to hold babies, change diapers and distinguish between eighteen different types of cries?

Of the six Jarrod children, Melissa and Erica were his only younger siblings. Which meant he didn't have a lot of experience with babies. Even being this close to one, with his mother right here, ready, willing and able to react to the baby's every need, made Trevor more than a bit uncomfortable.

Clearing his throat to cover the fact that he'd nearly taken a step back, away from the woman and her child, Trevor waited. She still owed him a name and an explanation for her presence, and he had work to do.

"My name is Haylie Smith."

He blinked, waiting for her to elaborate. Instead, after several long seconds ticked by, she tipped her head and let her eyes go wide, as though she'd just delivered a punch line. But he didn't get the joke.

"Haylie Smith," she said again, more firmly this time, careful to enunciate each syllable. "From Denver."

"I heard you," he murmured, fighting the twitch at the corner of his lips as they threatened to lift in an amused grin.

It wasn't often that he was treated like the slow kid in school. Very few would dare. Because while he was known to be fairly laid-back and fun-loving, even flirty at times when it came to women, he was also a Jarrod. One of the heirs to Donald Jarrod's vast fortune, and a successful entrepreneur in his own right.

He was rich, and he was powerful. And while it might take a lot to shake him from his easygoing nature, he wasn't a man other men wanted to risk pissing off.

That this stranger—a woman, no less—seemed to have no compunction about going nose-to-nose with him was more arousing than it should have been.

Not that she wasn't an attractive woman. At what he estimated to be about five feet four or five inches to his six-two, she was tall enough, but not too tall. She was also far from reed-thin, but nowhere near fat, either. She had curves in all the right places, pressing against the front of her sweater and filling out the hips of her slacks. The kind of figure that would feel soft and warm against his hard chest and firm thighs.

Her long, straight hair was like bottled sunshine and framed a heart-shaped face that was a fascinating mix of innocence and sensuality. The rosy bow of her mouth, the sharp, crystal-blue of her eyes, the way she held that baby with both confidence and possessiveness...

None of it should be turning him on, since he was about three seconds away from booting her out of his office, but damned if he wasn't starting to feel a telltale warmth in his blood and tightening in his gut.

Unfortunately—or maybe fortunately—she didn't seem to be suffering the same physiological response to him.

"I've been calling you for the past two months," she charged impatiently. "Leaving messages that you apparently couldn't be bothered to return."

With a nod, he moved around her and took his rightful place behind his desk. "My secretary mentioned that. Although I can't understand what's so pressing if you weren't willing to leave details about why you wanted to speak with me."

Just as he'd intended, his near dismissal of her caused her to move back around to the front of his desk. She didn't sit, though, instead standing directly in front of him while she bounced her hip and wove back and forth in a calm, gentle motion he assumed was for the baby's benefit.

"Some things are better said in person. And I didn't think you would appreciate your secretary being privy to your personal business."

At that, his brows drew together and he dragged his attention from the folder on the desk in front of him to her glittering gaze.

"I'm sorry, but I've never seen or heard of you before. What kind of personal business could you possibly have with me?" He nearly scoffed, wondering if this woman might be slightly unhinged. Maybe she'd convinced herself she was yet another long-lost Jarrod heir. Or maybe she'd seen one too many photographs of him in the local and national tabloids, and had convinced herself that she was one of his many feminine conquests.

He was debating the wisdom of getting up to open the double doors again, and possibly even buzzing for hotel security, when she switched the baby from one hip to the other and began to round his desk again—in the opposite direction this time—with slow, determined steps.

"You're right, you don't know me. We've never met. But a year ago, you met my sister, and from what I've heard, the two of you had a heck of a good time."

She stopped in front of him, towering over him in a manner he *definitely* didn't appreciate. He sat back, prepared to launch to his feet and stare her down, if necessary, but her next words glued him in place.

"And maybe if you returned a phone call once in a while, it wouldn't have taken me two months to track you down and introduce you to your son."

With that, she plopped the baby unceremoniously on his lap before leaning back to cross her arms beneath her breasts and look down at him with what could only be described as a satisfied smirk.

Two

Haylie really shouldn't have taken so much pleasure in Trevor Jarrod's shocked reaction to her pronouncement, but she did. His eyes flashed wide, his mouth dropped open like a guppy's and his hands on either side of Bradley's pudgy little body made him look as if he were juggling a ticking time bomb instead of a four-month-old infant.

She had to give Trevor credit, though. The minute she'd plopped Bradley on his lap and stepped away, Trevor's arms had come up to balance the child on his lap and keep the baby from toppling over.

After a few seconds of dead silence, Trevor seemed to regain a bit of his equilibrium. Snapping his mouth shut, he licked his lips and pushed to his feet, holding Bradley out in front of him. Apparently sensing Trevor's discomfort and nerves, the baby's legs started to kick and his face started to scrunch up and turn red.

Haylie stepped forward immediately and took the baby back, her pseudo-maternal instincts kicking in at the first sign of Bradley's distress. Cradling him against her chest, she patted his back and bounced gently up and down. In seconds, he was once again calm and content.

Trevor, however, looked anything but. His face had fallen into a hard, angry mask, his mouth thinning into a tight, flat line.

"I don't know what kind of game you think you're playing," he told her, his tone as cold as his coffee-brown eyes, "but I'm not amused. I'm afraid I'm going to have to ask you to leave before I'm forced to call security."

He was already moving around his desk and toward the double oak doors, so he didn't see her roll her eyes at his overly dramatic he-man speech.

He certainly wasn't going to need security to get rid of her. She would be more than happy to leave under her own steam.

In fact, if she didn't feel so strongly that a man deserved to know he was a father, and that a child deserved to know his only remaining parent, she wouldn't be in Aspen at all. She would be back home in Denver, minding her own business and doing her best to raise her nephew.

Not for the first time, Haylie cursed her sister's carefree, irresponsible nature. It had been Heather's place to find Trevor after their one-night stand and tell him she was pregnant. Her place to inform him that he had a son after Bradley had been born.

But, of course, her sister hadn't done either of those things. Oh, no, that would have been responsible and mature and right, a sign that she was finally growing up and might actually be ready to raise a child.

Haylie honestly didn't know what had been going

through her sister's head those long months of her pregnancy. Most of the time, Haylie had gotten the impression that the fact that she was a soon-to-be mother hadn't really sunken in for Heather. She'd gone about her business almost as though nothing in her life had changed except her belt size.

To the best of Haylie's knowledge, Heather *had* stopped drinking and smoking, and she'd cut down on her penchant for partying once her growing belly had put a bit of a damper on the fun of that, but otherwise, Heather had gone through those nine months with her head in the clouds.

Boy, talk about the cold slap of reality. Haylie didn't think she'd ever seen anyone so surprised as her sister when she'd gone into labor. And for the first couple of weeks after Bradley's birth, Haylie had actually thought Heather was growing up. Was going to step up to the plate and be a good, loving, *reliable* parent.

As usual when it came to her younger sister, however, the show of sensibility had been as fleeting as a summer storm. Before Bradley was a month old, Heather had started falling into her predictable, selfish habits. Staying out all night and sleeping well into the afternoon...not paying her bills...and worst of all, ignoring Bradley.

Despite her many shortcomings, Haylie loved her sister, but as far as Haylie was concerned, the last had been nearly unforgivable.

Bradley wasn't Haylie's child, but from the moment he'd come into the world, she'd loved him with an intensity that made her understand a mama bear's fierce instinct to protect her young. It was inconceivable to her that her sister—Bradley's *biological mother*—didn't share the same deep, powerful feelings for her own son.

But the point was moot, Haylie supposed. It was

her job now to protect and care for Bradley, and if she didn't love the little boy so much, if she didn't think he deserved the very best of everything and believe to the depth of her soul that he had the right to know his father—and that his father had the right to know him—she wouldn't be at Jarrod Ridge right now, in Trevor Jarrod's office, facing down a man who could not only have her thrown out of his family's resort, but possibly barred from the entire state of Colorado.

"You can call anyone you like," she told him, her tone much more cool, calm and collected than she felt, "but it won't change my reason for being here."

Carrying Bradley to one of the guest chairs in front of the desk, she started rooting in her purse with her free hand, then straightened, holding a small sheaf of papers. She crossed to Trevor, who was clutching the curved gold door handle in his long, bronzed fingers, but hadn't yet opened the door. She offered him a photo from the top of the stack.

"This is my sister, Heather," she murmured, then had to swallow when her voice grew thick and tears threatened.

At least Trevor was looking at the photograph, actually studying her sister's features rather than dismissing her out of hand. But as he lifted his head and their eyes met, Haylie knew he had no recollection whatsoever of meeting and sleeping with Heather.

With a mental sigh, she swallowed again and licked her lips before continuing. "You apparently met her while in Denver on business, at one of the clubs downtown. Heather was a beautiful young woman, but she liked to party. And she *didn't* like to go home alone."

Something flickered in the depths of his dark sable eyes, and he said, "Was?"

Haylie's chest hitched as she gave a shaky nod and handed him the newspaper clipping she'd brought along with Heather's picture. "She was killed in a car accident two months ago."

Her chest tightened even more when a look of genuine sympathy passed over his features. He might not remember Heather, and he might suspect Haylie was up to no good with her *it's a boy!* announcement, but he didn't appear to be completely cold and heartless.

"I know you probably think I'm trying to work some elaborate scam on you. Or that I'm hoping to snag a bit of the Jarrod fortune for myself. But I assure you, that isn't the case."

Bradley started to fuss, and she jiggled him slightly, transferring him to her other hip. "I'm only here because Heather told me you're Bradley's father, and since she never got around to contacting you herself, I felt it was my place to let you know she'd passed away, and that you have a child. More importantly, I think he—" she lifted Bradley, making it clear to whom she was referring "—deserves to know his father and where he comes from on his father's side."

When Trevor didn't respond, she slipped the photograph and obituary out of his loose grasp. "So check me out if you need to. Draw up whatever legal documents you feel are fair and will protect your assets. But don't punish your son for his mother's mistakes."

Trevor's grip tightened on the door handle while he studied the woman standing before him. He'd met his fair share of young ladies with dollar signs in their eyes and their sights set on the Jarrod millions, and had become adept at brushing them off.

But none of his usual gold digger alarm bells were

going off with Haylie Smith. Something about her told him she was sincere. Even if she was wrong about the baby's paternity, it was clear she *believed* what she was saying—or at least what her sister had apparently told her before her death.

Glancing down at the photograph clutched in Haylie's white-knuckled fingers, he once again racked his brain for any memory of the woman he'd supposedly spent a less-than-memorable night with. He remembered the trip to Denver, and even stopping in at one of the city's more popular nightclubs for a drink after a day filled with disappointing meetings and a potentially lucrative business venture that had fallen through. He'd been frustrated and annoyed, and had needed to blow off some steam.

The earsplitting techno music had rattled his brain, but he'd stuck around long enough to down a few drinks. And he remembered women...lots of women in short skirts and ice-pick stilettos, both out on the dance floor and crowded into booths the color of Hpnotiq vodka. Several had hit on him, but he hadn't been in the mood.

Or maybe, after a few more drinks, he had.

There was no recollection there, though. The only thing he found familiar about the woman in the picture came from her resemblance to the woman standing in front of him now. They had the same blue eyes and honey-blond hair, the same bow-tie mouth and long, thick lashes. But that's where the similarities ended.

Where Heather's hair was styled in a bold, spikey do, with a streak of magenta running down one side, Haylie's fell soft and naturally around her face and looked infinitely touchable.

Where Heather's lips were painted a bright, shocking

shade of pink, Haylie wore nothing but a layer of clear gloss.

And where Heather's eyes appeared hard and jaded, Haylie's were deep pools of warmth and earnestness.

How could two women—sisters—with so many of the same features look so very different? he wondered.

He also wondered how one sister could go nine-plus months without making a single effort to inform a man he was allegedly going to be a father, while the other had spent two months trying to track him down by phone and felt so strongly about her duty to inform him of his parenthood—again, *alleged* parenthood—that she'd driven nearly four hours from Denver to Aspen with a baby in tow and wheedled her way into his office just to confront him.

For that reason alone, he found himself wanting to know if her allegations were true. And if they were... Well, he wanted to know for himself if she was right about the child in her arms being his.

He wasn't sure how he felt about the possibility of being a father. The very thought made his stomach clench and his chest grow tight. But not with any innate paternal sentiments. No, what he was feeling was much more along the lines of dread and panic.

At only twenty-seven, the notion of getting married and starting a family had never crossed his mind. And the idea of having a child dropped in his lap out of the blue had been even further behind.

He was too busy enjoying his life, sowing wild oats and working to build his marketing company. Add to that the more recent turn of events that had made him the president of marketing at Jarrod Ridge, and he barely had time to hike, to ski, to *breathe,* let alone raise a child.

There was no point worrying about that or projecting into the future, though, until he knew for certain.

Releasing the door handle, he returned to his desk. Much more of this stalking back and forth and the carpet would need to be replaced.

As he lowered himself into his chair and reached for the phone, he gestured for Haylie to take a seat.

"Diana," he said the minute his secretary picked up. "Get Dr. Lazlo on the line for me, please."

Once she'd answered in the affirmative, he hung up and leaned his arms on the desk. He looked at the baby on Haylie's lap, searching for signs that this was, indeed, his child, but all he saw was…a baby.

He didn't see his eyes or his hair or his smile, didn't see *Jarrod bloodlines* stamped on every inch of that pale, pudgy baby skin.

Did that mean the child…Bradley, his name was Bradley. Did that mean Bradley *wasn't* his…or simply that a four-month-old's parentage couldn't be determined just by looking?

Lifting his gaze, Trevor pinned Haylie with a hard stare. "We'll have a paternity test run immediately. And God help you if your story is a lie."

He wasn't sure what he would do, exactly, but the very thought that she was trying to get one over on him made his jaw lock and his temperature rise. On the desk in front of him, his fists clenched until his knuckles cracked.

If this whole thing turned out to be some crazy fabrication in a bid to get money or besmirch his good name—his family's good name—he *was not* going to be happy. The Jarrods had Erica's fiancé and longtime family attorney Christian, as well as a bevy of other legal eagles on retainer, who would have no problem racking up billable hours devising new and creative ways to make Haylie Smith sorry she had ever come to Jarrod Ridge.

At his veiled threat, he'd half expected her to blink. To decide that maybe this charade wasn't the wisest plan of action, after all.

But once again, he'd underestimated her. Not only didn't she blink—figuratively or literally—but her expression remained just as firm and determined.

"If he's not your baby," she said softly, "it won't be my lie, it will be my sister's."

As the minutes crawled by, with Trevor Jarrod staring her down like an opponent in a boxing ring, the silence in the luxurious office was thick enough to carve with a knife. There was no fire crackling in the hearth behind him, and no office noises filtering in from the other side of the wide double doors. Only the rhythmic ticking of the clock on the far wall and Bradley's occasional contented gurgle and sucking on his tiny fist kept her from hearing her own heart pounding beneath her ribs.

She could certainly understand Trevor's anger and suspicions. In his shoes, she would be thinking and feeling the exact same way.

But she was not the bad guy here. In fact, she was being an excessively *good guy* by bringing Bradley to Jarrod Ridge at all. She could have just as easily remained in Denver and raised her sister's child as her own.

It wasn't as if Trevor would have known the difference. Up until now, he hadn't been aware of Bradley's existence, and she sincerely doubted he'd have been struck by a sudden twinge of conscience and returned to Denver to see if he'd left behind any stray, fatherless progeny as a result of his numerous one-night stands in the Mile High City.

And she didn't even have a deathbed promise to her sister hanging over her head, prompting her to do the right thing by both Bradley and Trevor. Given the fact that Heather had claimed several times that she would tell Trevor about the baby or had been trying to contact him to do just that…and that she very obviously hadn't done anything of the sort…Haylie was only following her own strict moral code, which dictated that a man had the right to know he'd fathered a child.

Whether or not he stepped up and took responsibility for that child was a different story, but he had the right to know, and Haylie's own conscience wouldn't have let her go much longer without making sure that he did.

If it turned out Trevor wasn't Bradley's father… Well, she couldn't very well go back in time and strangle her sister, but she sure would be tempted. The best she could do, she supposed, was apologize for the misunderstanding and any inconvenience she'd caused him and go back to Denver to do what she'd planned all along—raise Bradley on her own.

Before either of them could form words to break the Mexican standoff between their cool, targeted gazes, the phone on Trevor's desk buzzed. He grabbed the handset and listened, presumably to whatever his assistant had to say.

"Thank you," he murmured, and a moment later, "Dr. Lazlo, Trevor Jarrod. I've got a situation here that requires the utmost discretion."

After a pause in which the physician was likely raising a hand, swearing on both his Hippocratic oath and a stack of Bibles, Trevor continued, "How long will it take to get results on a paternity test?"

A small frown marred his brow, and Haylie raised one of her own. Obviously any response other than "instantaneously" didn't set well with Mr. Jarrod.

"Very well, although if there's any way to rush that and still maintain accuracy…" More silence while the person on the other end spoke, too low for her to hear. "We can be at your office in thirty minutes."

With a nod, Trevor thanked the doctor for his time and hung up before turning his dark stare back to her… and the baby on her lap.

"We're driving into the city to have blood tests done," he told her, as though she hadn't heard every word of his side of the conversation. And his tone left no room for argument, even if she'd cared to make one. "Now."

Pushing up from his desk, he came around, no doubt expecting her to hop up and follow him like a well-trained puppy. Instead, she pushed slowly to her feet, shifting Bradley around to her front as she strode slowly across the office to one of the soft-as-butter leather sofas lining the side walls.

"What are you doing?" Trevor asked crossly. In her peripheral vision, she saw him fold his arms over his wide chest and tap the toe of one fawn-colored boot in annoyance.

"I'm changing Bradley's diaper before I stuff him back into his snowsuit," she told Trevor calmly, laying the baby down and beginning to unsnap the legs of his denim overalls. But before she removed the soiled diaper, she tipped her head meaningfully in Trevor's direction. "Unless you'd prefer to drive all the way to the doctor's office with the windows down."

Mouth flattening into a thin, unhappy line, he

dropped his arms and stuffed his hands into the front pockets of his jeans instead. "No, go ahead."

Biting back a gloating chuckle, she returned her attention to Bradley and quickly finished cleaning him up, then got him tucked into his thick, baby-blue snowsuit. When she tightened the faux-fur-lined hood around his face, he grinned and kicked his little legs, and she couldn't resist leaning in to flick his nose and grin back.

Then, remembering that Trevor was still in the room, watching them like a hawk, she cleared her throat and straightened somewhat self-consciously.

"Almost ready," she said, standing to put on her own sage-green parka before gathering Bradley and reaching for the strap of his diaper bag.

Trevor was suddenly there, grabbing it for her. "I've got it."

She swallowed again, this time because the intensity of his dark gaze had her cheeks going hot and her stomach swooping like a roller coaster on the downslide.

"Thank you," she managed, following quietly behind him when he moved to the office door, opened it and stepped into the reception area.

His secretary lifted her head at her boss's approach, but her glance skated quickly past Trevor to eye Haylie and Bradley. Haylie didn't think the woman had heard anything that had been said behind the closed office doors, but it was obvious she was curious about who exactly Haylie was, what she'd needed to talk to Trevor about and why she'd brought a four-month-old along to do it. But like all good secretaries, she was discreet, keeping her mouth shut and waiting until her employer told her what he needed.

"Diana, I'm going to be out of the office for a while,"

Trevor informed her, not bothering to introduce Haylie, even though it was clear that wherever he was going, she was tagging along. "Possibly the rest of the day. Reschedule any meetings for me, please, and field anything else that comes up."

"Yes, sir," Diana responded, jotting a note on her desk blotter before taking to her keyboard to bring up what Haylie assumed was Trevor's daily schedule.

From a hidden closet behind the receptionist's desk, Trevor pulled out his coat and shrugged it on. Stuffing his hands into the pockets, he pulled out a cell phone, checked the display and put it back.

"My cell will be on if you need to reach me," he added, "but—"

"—Try not to need you," Diana finished for him.

He flashed a quick half smile. "Right."

Lifting his gaze to Haylie's, he met her eyes for a second, then said, "Ready?"

She nodded, passing the reception desk to once again trail after the man who was—for the moment, at least—in charge. But instead of taking the lead, this time he held the door and ushered her and Bradley ahead of him. An act of chivalry that for some reason had her tightening her grip on her nephew and reminding herself that she didn't fall into bed with every handsome man she met the way her sister always had. If anything, while she was in Trevor Jarrod's presence, she needed to be even more diligent about disengaging her female hormones and keeping her wits about her.

But if Haylie were honest with herself, she would have to admit that, not for the first time since meeting Bradley's father, she couldn't quite blame her sister any longer for having a one-night stand with this man. If Haylie were a bit more extroverted, a bit less timid when it came to flirting with the opposite sex and had a bit more time on her hands to actually meet people of the opposite sex, she suspected she'd be tempted to fall into bed with him, too.

Three

The trip to Dr. Lazlo's office took closer to forty-five minutes than thirty, mostly due to the fact that Trevor had never been around a child and had no idea how much paraphernalia they required just to get from point A to point B.

First, he'd led Haylie through one of the Manor's side exits to his fire-engine-red Hummer parked in a reserved spot in the employee parking lot. Only to have her arch a brow and refuse to get in on the passenger side until they'd collected Bradley's car seat from her vehicle.

So they'd tromped back to the Manor—because she wouldn't get in with the baby, even to let him drive them around to her car—and through the main hallways of the hotel until they'd reached one of the more public entrances closer to the guest parking area.

Trevor would have preferred to simply walk around

the giant building, finding the light fall of snow and chill in the air bracing. But in the short time they'd been outdoors, Haylie's and Bradley's cheeks had already turned pink with cold, and Trevor didn't want to risk either of them getting sick or frostbitten, so he'd opted for taking the partially heated shortcut past God knew how many inquiring eyes.

As if having a strange woman pop up in his office with a baby she claimed to be his wasn't bad enough, the idea that someone might find out about this latest wrench in the works and splash it across the front page of every rag tabloid in Colorado and beyond was enough to give him an ulcer *and* high blood pressure. All he could do was hope that the people they passed were mere tourists and not some form of despicable paparazzi disguised as guests in an effort to dig up dirt on the Jarrods yet again.

All he needed was for the three of them to wend their way through the buzzing center of the main hotel and out to the parking lot without being waylaid by anyone who might be curious about Haylie's identity.

At least it didn't look as though he and Haylie were together. She was walking off to the side two paces behind him, and they weren't doing anything telling like holding hands. For all onlookers knew, he was simply showing a VIP guest to her lodge personally.

Although, he had to admit that the urge to reach out and clasp her hand *was* there.

Not because he was attracted to her. He gave a mental snort. Nothing as ridiculous as that.

No, it was just that she wasn't exactly wearing the most sensible winter boots. He doubted they had much tread on them at all, and the ground was slippery.

For that matter, the parts of the resort's flooring that

weren't covered in rugs or carpeting could be slippery if they got wet, too. It wasn't worth the risk of a lawsuit to have *anyone* fall and hurt themselves on Jarrod Ridge property, and he certainly didn't want Haylie to lose her footing and chance dropping Bradley. Whether the baby turned out to be his or not, he would never want to see a child hurt.

They were halfway across the lobby, exit in sight, and he thought they might just make it.

And...no such luck. Trevor gave a low curse beneath his breath as he saw his brother Guy bearing down on them.

Guy was their other brother Blake's fraternal twin, as well as Jarrod Ridge's main restaurateur-slash-food guru. Or as the Jarrod boys liked to tease, their chief cook and bottle washer. The resort boasted four restaurants and six bars, all of which Guy helped to oversee.

Food might be Guy's specialty, but because Trevor was in charge of resort-wide marketing, most publicity related to the restaurants fell under his umbrella. And though their largest public affair—the Food and Wine Gala—was behind them for another year, that didn't mean they weren't constantly working on other events, tossing around other ideas.

At the moment, he and Guy were trying to organize specialty menus and advertising for a sort of "world tour" of the Manor's eateries. Chagall's would cover a taste of France, Emilio's would cover a taste of Italy, The Golden Palace would cover a taste of China, and so on.

Guy could have picked a better time to bother him about it, though.

Stopping in his tracks—in the middle of the damn lobby, no less—Trevor braced himself for Guy's approach and prayed Haylie would have the sense to keep her mouth shut.

"Hey," his brother greeted him.

Three years older than Trevor and only an inch or so shorter, he was dressed in black slacks and a plain white button-down shirt. Casual, and yet not quite as casual as Trevor's current post-ski-slope attire.

His brown hair, which he normally wore a bit long and unkempt, was cut short and neatly styled. Avery's doing, no doubt. As were the new clothes and the twinkle that never seemed to leave his brother's eyes these days. Trevor liked Guy's new fiancée, but the fact that she so obviously loved his brother and was having such a positive influence on him in every way only made Trevor respect her all the more.

"Hey," he murmured back. And just as he'd expected, Guy unrolled a sheaf of oversize papers he'd been carrying under his arm.

"I've been looking over the poster mock-ups, and there are a few changes I'd like to make. Especially to the proposed menus." One corner of his mouth lifted in a grin and he winked. "You know how I am when it comes to food. Do you have a minute to discuss it?"

"Actually, now isn't a good time," Trevor replied honestly. "Can I catch you later?"

Since Trevor was all about marketing and almost never unavailable when he was at the Ridge and in full business mode, his brother's raised brows came as no surprise. Then Guy happened to glance over his shoulder, to where Haylie was standing just behind him, still holding a powder-blue, near mummified Bradley. There was no denying that she was with Trevor, patiently waiting for him to finish his conversation so they could carry on.

"Oh, yeah," Guy muttered. "Sure."

From the expression on Guy's face, Trevor knew he was curious, that he was dying to ask about the pretty woman and her baby. Thankfully, he was wise enough to keep his mouth shut. At least for the moment. Of course, the family grapevine ran at the speed of light, so Trevor had no illusions that word of his mysterious companion wouldn't get around. Dammit.

And then Guy went and made matters even worse. Stretching an arm past Trevor's impeding bulk, he offered Haylie his hand.

"Guy Jarrod," he said by way of introduction. "Trevor's older brother. Older, smarter and more handsome, of course," he added with a wink. This time, it was meant to be charismatic, not self-deprecating.

Trevor rolled his eyes, as much at Guy's display of chivalry as at the fact that things seemed to be getting dicier for him by the second.

Haylie accepted Guy's hand and gave it a polite shake. "Haylie Smith," she offered. Nothing more, nothing less. Thank goodness.

While she was perfectly courteous, Trevor noticed she didn't seem the least impressed by his brother's attempt at charm. For some reason, that pleased him. Not that it mattered one way or the other—Guy was very happily and very firmly engaged, and Trevor wasn't interested in any woman who came with even a hint of strings **attached**.

And **Haylie** came with enough strings to knit an afghan.

"Look," Trevor said to his brother, doing his best to tamp down his growing impatience. "We're in kind of a hurry. I'll talk to you later, all right?"

With that, he tilted his head, silently gesturing for Haylie to move ahead of him toward the nearest exit.

"Right. Fine. Later," Guy mumbled as they stepped away.

Trevor felt his brother's gaze on his back the entire time, and knew his mind must be racing. Dammit, just what he needed—more attention drawn to Haylie's presence and his peculiar behavior.

Against his better judgment, as soon as they stepped outside into the brisk December chill, Trevor gave in to the voice in his head that kept telling him to reach out and touch her.

But he didn't take her hand. Too intimate and not his place. Instead, he took her elbow, just to steady her and avoid any accidents while they made their way to her car.

She didn't seem startled by the action, even shooting him a small smile over Bradley's fuzzy, hooded head.

"Your brother seems nice," she said, and he knew she was just trying to make small talk.

"Yeah" was his monosyllabic response.

Sure, Guy was nice. Nice and curious, no doubt.

Haylie's car, as it turned out, was another cause for concern. Though it was several years old and a model he was pretty sure had been taken off the market, it looked to be in good enough shape. Except for the tires.

How could anyone live in Colorado and not have snow tires on their vehicle by the time the weather turned icy? Or if they were snow tires, the tread was so worn that they might as well have been inner tubes.

None of his business, Trevor told himself while Haylie dug into her purse for her keys. Unless, of course, it turned out that Bradley *was* his son. In which case, it was very much his business, and he would see to it that all four of the woman's tires were replaced immediately. Or better yet, he would replace her car entirely…buy her something much safer and better suited to Aspen and Denver in the winter months. A Hummer like his. Or maybe a damn tank.

Juggling her purse and keys and the baby, Haylie struggled to get the driver's side door open, and Trevor stepped forward to help.

"Here, let me," he murmured, taking the keys from her hand.

Once he had the car unlocked, she opened the rear door, then turned to him and said, "Could you hold him for a minute?"

Without waiting for a response, she thrust Bradley against his chest and his arms came up automatically to grab the overstuffed bundle shoved in his direction. Catching the baby beneath the arms, Trevor held him out away from him like a bag of angry, venomous snakes.

Haylie was facing the opposite direction, fiddling with the child's safety seat and the belts that held it in place, so she didn't see what he was sure was an expression of sheer terror on his face.

He didn't know anything about babies. Not how to hold them or feed them or change a diaper. What if Bradley started crying? And didn't babies leak? Tears and drool and spit-up, and even worse things that, thank God, a diaper would likely catch.

But Bradley wasn't leaking. If anything, he looked positively delighted by his new handler. His cheeks were pudgy and pink, his eyes bright with amusement. He was kicking his little legs as though dancing to music only he could hear, and if Trevor wasn't mistaken, he thought the child might even be smiling.

Did babies this age smile, or did he just have gas?

Bradley gave an extra-exuberant kick and giggled. Intentionally. Definitely not gastrointestinal related.

With a silent chuckle of his own, Trevor's trepidation began to fade and he bent his arms, bringing Bradley back against his chest.

He was kind of a cute kid. Didn't mean he was a Jarrod, but he still had that whole irresistible baby thing going on that Trevor had heard so much about, especially where women and their biological clocks were concerned.

A minute or two later, when Haylie climbed out of the car with the safety seat, Trevor was making faces at Bradley and bouncing up and down the way he'd seen her do back in his office.

"I can take him now," she said.

Trevor shook his head. "That's okay, I've got him."

After all, this wasn't as tough as he'd thought, and if the baby turned out not to be his, it might be the only chance he got to do the new-dad thing for quite some time. And if Bradley *did* turn out to be his son…well, he could use all the practice he could get.

Sliding his glance to Haylie, he nodded at the car seat. "Can you get that, or do you want me to carry it?"

"I can get it, but…" She frowned a bit and sounded slightly worried. "Are you sure you wouldn't rather trade?"

"Nope, we're fine," he said, giving Bradley another little jiggle that had him giggling. "Make sure your car is locked and that you have everything you need before we take off."

Half an hour after *that,* Trevor pulled the Hummer into a spot in front of the doctor's office and cut the engine. Haylie was already out of the car and working to collect Bradley when he got around to her side to help.

Unlike while Trevor had been holding him, the little boy's nose was now wrinkled, his mouth pursed and his eyes squinted in displeasure. He was wiggling and whimpering, and the pink in his cheeks definitely didn't have anything to do with the cold.

"What's wrong with him?" Trevor asked, trying not to let his concern slip into his tone.

"He's just fussy," Haylie replied, lifting the child from the car seat and shouldering him at the same time she hefted the bulging diaper bag with its yellow giraffe and purple hippopotamus.

Trevor took the bag for her and closed the door before they started up the sidewalk in front of the tall redbrick building.

"Can you get a bottle out of there?" she asked, pointing to one of the bag's side pockets. "He's probably hungry, and after that he'll need a new diaper and then a nap. I hope this doesn't take too long, or we're going to have one very loud, unhappy baby on our hands. Unless he sleeps through the whole thing. That would be nice."

A loud, unhappy baby didn't sound like something Trevor cared to experience. Unfortunately, DNA tests tended to involve needles and poking, which he didn't think would do much to improve Bradley's current disposition.

Entering the office, he left Haylie to find a seat and give Bradley his bottle while he let the receptionist know in a whispered voice who he was and why they were here.

It didn't take long for the nurse to call them back and lead them to a private exam room, where the baby continued to empty his bottle, his lashes fluttering as his eyes grew heavier and heavier. Moments later, the doctor arrived, greeting Trevor and introducing himself to Haylie. After a brief examination of Bradley, who had finished his bottle and was now sound asleep in Haylie's arms, the doctor pushed his stool back and regarded both adults.

"It's my understanding that you'd like a paternity test to determine that the child is..."

Dr. Lazlo let the sentence trail off, and Haylie quickly supplied, "His," with a tilt of her head in Trevor's direction.

"Bradley is my sister's son," she continued to explain. "Heather passed away two months ago in an auto accident, without informing Mr. Jarrod that he was a father. Mr. Jarrod wants to be sure I'm telling him the truth about Bradley's parentage and didn't come to Jarrod Ridge to pan for gold with a baby and a well-constructed story."

Trevor shot her an annoyed glance, leaning back against the high countertop to cross his arms over his chest. "That's probably more than the good doctor needs to know," he pointed out.

The doctor gave a friendly chuckle. "Not to worry. I've conducted thousands of these tests, and I assure you, I'm very discreet. I'll handle your samples and the results personally, and send them to the lab under fictitious names."

Trevor inclined his head in approval, but he still wasn't happy. Bad enough they were here at all—he really didn't need the entire situation spelled out for him again, or for relative strangers.

"Now," the physician said, resting his hands on his knees. "There are two types of paternity tests. Both have long, hard-to-pronounce medical names that I'm sure you don't care about, but suffice to say that one, PCR, involves swabbing the inside of the cheek, the other, RFLP, drawing blood."

"Which is more accurate?" Trevor wanted to know.

"RFLP, the blood sample. We can do both, if you like. Each test is fairly accurate, but with both there would be very little doubt as to the child's paternity."

Cocking his head, Trevor turned to look at Haylie. She stared up at him, her eyes and face telling him nothing of her inner thoughts.

"Would you mind if we did both?" he asked. "To be certain."

She was silent for several seconds, then lifted one slim shoulder in a shrug. "It's all right with me, but the blood test is definitely going to wake Bradley, and he is *definitely* going to shatter some eardrums."

"We'll start with the buccal swab," the doctor told her, "and I'll be as gentle as possible."

Twenty minutes later, Bradley was once again sound asleep, this time in the backseat of Trevor's Hummer as they headed back to Jarrod Ridge. The needle prick had woken him, just as Haylie warned it would, and he'd shrieked at the top of his lungs for a good three minutes. But after that, he'd wound down to a few ragged whimpers before drifting off again against Haylie's shoulder.

Breaking the silence inside the car, Trevor murmured, "The doctor said the test results could take a couple of weeks, depending on how backed up the lab is."

She nodded, twisting in her seat to look at him rather than out the window. "I think he's right about not putting a rush on it. You want to keep this quiet until you know for sure whether Bradley is your son, and that would only rouse suspicions."

"I believe Dr. Lazlo will be as discreet as possible,"

he agreed, "but things have a way of getting out, anyway, especially if employees get curious and start poking around."

"I don't mind waiting, if you don't. And I promise to be just as circumspect as the doctor. No one back home knows anything about you. I don't think they're even particularly curious about who Bradley's father might be." Her mouth turned down at the corners, eyes narrowing. "Heather had that kind of reputation. No one was surprised when she turned up pregnant without a man hanging around to claim the baby."

To Trevor, she sounded slightly embarrassed by that fact, as well as disapproving, but also...defensive. As though she hadn't agreed with her sister's behavior, wouldn't have chosen that sort of lifestyle for either of them, but would stick up for Heather no matter what. Even now that she was gone.

He couldn't fault her for that. As it turned out, he had one sister more than he'd known about while growing up, but that didn't keep him from feeling protective of both his full sister, Melissa, and his recently discovered half sister, Erica.

For that matter, he felt protective of his entire family. The Jarrods were sort of like the Three Musketeers—all for one and one for all.

None of them were perfect, but despite their mistakes and the occasional flaw in their personalities, he would still defend any one of them to the death. That Haylie felt the same way about her sister—and her sister's child—didn't surprise him.

"That's something else we need to talk about, actually."

"What?" she asked, her brows drawing down in confusion.

"Where you'll be staying until the test results are in."

"Oh. That's no problem. As soon as we get back to your office, I'll give you my address and phone number, all the ways to reach me. You're welcome to visit Bradley anytime, if you like. Although, if you'd rather not until you know for sure...I'll understand," she finished quietly.

Understand, but not necessarily approve, he thought with some amusement.

Not that it mattered.

"That's not what I meant," he told her.

"I'm sorry. What did you mean then?"

"I've been giving it some thought, and until we know for sure whether or not Bradley is my son, I'd like the two of you to move in with me."

Four

For long minutes, Haylie was too stunned to respond. She sat there in the passenger seat of Trevor's SUV with her mouth hanging open. Catching flies, as her mother used to say. But she couldn't have been more surprised if he'd announced he wanted to give up his family's millions and go to work as a fry cook at a fast-food restaurant.

Shifting around to face him more fully, she wiggled inside of her overstuffed parka, loosening the zipper in an effort to cool down and breathe a bit more easily. The heating vents were blowing, but she didn't think they were the reason she was suddenly feeling flushed.

No, that would be confusion mixed with a fair dose of alarm.

After swallowing a couple of times and barely resisting the urge to squiggle her ears to make sure she hadn't misheard him, she managed to utter two rather strangled words. "Excuse me?"

Without taking his eyes off the road, he said, "I think it's best for everyone involved."

She *really* wanted to slap her ears and make sure she was hearing him correctly, because nothing he was saying seemed to make sense. Swallowing again, she cleared her throat and asked, "How so?"

He shrugged one broad shoulder, made even broader by the thickness of his coat. "If Bradley is mine, then I've got some lost time to make up for. I'd prefer to keep him close by, start getting to know him...and get used to being a father."

His voice tightened with his last few words, as though the thought that he might truly be the father of a little boy he'd known nothing about until a couple of hours ago was something he'd prefer not to think about.

Too bad said little boy was sleeping in the backseat at that very moment. And while Haylie certainly didn't have the kind of money to gamble with that Trevor Jarrod had, she'd have been willing to bet the DNA tests would come out with a glaring "Congratulations, Daddy!" message stamped all over them.

"I can understand that," she agreed, "but it won't take *that* long for the paternity results to come in. And Bradley is already four months old—surely another couple of weeks won't make that much difference. Besides, I have a life back in Denver. A business to run. I can't just pick up and disappear."

"Then leave the boy with me. You've had four months with him, I've had barely a day. And I have plenty of room, as well as the money to hire a round-the-clock nanny."

Haylie's eyes went wide. She'd never considered

herself a violent person, but right that second she was extremely tempted to reach out and slap the man sitting beside her. There were so many things wrong with what he'd just said, she didn't know where to begin.

The boy? A nanny?

Leave Bradley with Trevor?

"Absolutely not."

This time, it was her voice that came out strained, but not due to nerves. Oh, no, hers was all temper. She was skating past mere anger, headed deep into furious territory.

"I may not be Bradley's biological mother, but I'm the only mother he's known for the past two months—and quite a bit before that, if the truth be known. There is *no way* I would leave him *anywhere,* with *anyone.*"

The waterproof material of her jacket made a slick scratching sound as she crossed her arms. "I don't care if you are his father," she muttered with no small amount of aversion to the word.

What was that saying about no good deed going unpunished? Boy, was she being smacked in the face with its meaning now.

All she'd wanted was to do the right thing. To let a man know he'd fathered a child with a woman who never would have told him on her own, and whom he never would have run into again otherwise.

She'd wanted to do the right thing by Bradley. He was a Jarrod, after all. And even though she didn't need the family's millions, didn't believe a child needed that kind of money to grow up happy and healthy and well-loved, he still deserved to know where he came from, who his ancestors were.

But *no good deed…* And here she was, only a handful

of hours past her "good deed," and it was already biting her in the butt.

For several seconds, Trevor didn't reply. Then his low voice carried over the short distance separating them, his words stopping her heart and freezing her blood.

"I could take him from you, you know."

Okay, so that hadn't been Argument Number One in Trevor's big plan to convince Haylie to move in with him for the next couple of weeks. But something about the way she'd gotten up on her hind legs about not leaving Bradley with him put him on the defensive.

On the one hand, he liked how protective she was of the infant. If the kid really did turn out to be his, he suspected he was going to have a lot of moments of feeling very grateful toward her for caring for his son the way she had.

Sure, Bradley was her nephew, so he knew there had to be a strong bond there. But from the sounds of it, Bradley's mother—this now-deceased Heather he had no recollection of ever meeting—had been a bit of a troublemaker. Or rather, gotten into her fair share of trouble.

It would have been easy, even understandable, for Haylie to cut her sister off and say no more. No more cleaning up her messes, no more coming to her rescue.

But Haylie hadn't done that, had she? No, she had not only stuck by her sister through all of her screwups, but had taken over the role of mother to her infant son after Heather's unexpected death.

For that, Haylie deserved a whole row of gold stars. And if he turned out to be Bradley's father, she would also have Trevor's undying gratitude.

"I'll fight you for him," she said through gritted teeth, breaking into his thoughts.

She sounded completely outraged, on the verge of doing him bodily damage, and his opinion of her ratcheted up another dozen notches.

Of course, she wouldn't have a chance in hell. She could fight him from now until doomsday, but if he wanted to take primary physical custody of the little boy in the backseat, he had both the lawyers and the resources to see that it was done. Even before the DNA results came in, the argument could be made that *she* had come to *him* with claims of his paternity and, given that the child's mother had kept both her pregnancy and the infant a secret from him…well, he imagined the courts would be only too happy to rectify the circumstances in his favor.

That *wasn't* the route he wanted to take, however, and was already regretting bringing it up. Instead, he preferred to finesse the situation. Something he was normally much better at.

Considering the baby bomb that had been dropped on him only hours ago, Trevor decided to cut himself some slack. He was still reeling from the first moment the words "here's your son" had slipped from Haylie's mouth, let alone everything that had been spinning through his head since.

And the fact was, he needed Haylie on his side. It wasn't easy for him to admit that, even to himself, but he knew *nothing* about kids. Little ones, big ones; they might as well have been tiny green creatures from the planet Krypton.

If Bradley turned out to be his flesh and blood, then no matter what Trevor had said about hiring a nanny, he was going to need her to teach him everything he needed to know about his own son. A nanny could change diapers and heat up bottles, but she wouldn't know Bradley's favorite brand of baby food, or whether he was ticklish or what made him laugh and cry.

Haylie knew those things. She'd spent the last four months learning all there was to know about his son.

Maybe his son.

His possible son.

No sense getting ahead of himself—or the paternity tests.

Still, the Jarrods were big on family, which meant that if he ended up with the right to lay claim to the baby, he would never dream of shutting Haylie out of Bradley's life. Bradley would need an aunt on his mother's side, as much as a father and aunts and uncles on Trevor's side.

So it would be smart to make Haylie his ally rather than his enemy. And better to start down that path sooner rather than later.

"Let's try to avoid the threats and talk of a custody battle altogether, shall we? At least for the time being. I think if you consider what I'm suggesting, you'll realize it's best for everyone involved."

When he cast a quick glance in Haylie's direction, he found her staring at him, one brow raised.

"Really?" she asked, sarcasm heavy in her tone. "How do you figure that?"

With a shrug, he returned his attention to the road. "Like I said, it's only for a few weeks, and it will give Bradley and me a chance to get to know each other." No, that didn't sound quite right. What was a better word for getting acquainted with your possible progeny? "To bond."

From the corner of his eye, he saw her lips thin in

what he thought was reluctant approval. He'd gotten one right, then...and annoyed Haylie in the process.

"What about me?" she asked, her gaze focused straight ahead through the windshield, just like his.

He frowned. "What about you? I already said that you and Bradley can move into my home together. I've got plenty of space, if that's what you're worried about. The two of you can have your own room and have the run of the place during the day while I'm at the resort."

"And what about my life back home? I do have a job, you know. A business to run, employees to oversee, a schedule to keep."

He shook his head and readjusted his hands on the steering wheel. "I'm sorry," he said. "What is it that you do?"

He couldn't believe he hadn't wondered about that before now. Chalk it up to yet another sign of his complete and utter shock at having a four-month-old child dropped in his lap. Literally.

Now that the topic had been brought up, however, he realized a background check wouldn't be out of the question. As soon as he returned to the office, he would make some phone calls and find the best person to do a bit of very *quiet* digging into Haylie's life, both the professional and private sides.

As long as they were at it, he'd see what they could learn about the sister, too. She might be deceased, but a good investigator should at least be able to determine whether Heather had actually been in Denver at the same time as Trevor's visit. If she truly had frequented the club where Haylie claimed he and Heather had met, and if there were any other candidates for fatherhood lurking in the shadows.

And even before Dr. Lazlo called with the paternity

results, a background check would give him an idea of Haylie's financial situation. Whether it was more or less likely that she was using her dead sister's child to wring a few of the Jarrod family's millions from him.

"I'm an event planner," Haylie supplied, oblivious to the thoughts and plans spiraling silently through his head.

"And you own your own company?" he encouraged.

She nodded. "A small one. I only have a handful of helpers, but the holidays are a busy time for us. I can barely afford to be away overnight, let alone for a week or two."

Ignoring the last part of her statement—temporarily, at least—Trevor asked, "What's the business called?"

Apparently, he was being too nice all of a sudden, because she cast him a suspicious glance before answering.

"It's Your Party."

"Cute," he murmured, an idea springing to mind and starting to take shape.

"Thank you."

"Do you specialize in anything in particular?"

"Not really," she admitted. "Or not yet. It's only been three years since we opened our doors, so we're still finding our footing and working to build a reputation as Denver's go-to event-planning company."

"Bet you're dealing with a lot of upcoming Christmas party preparations, huh?"

"Definitely. November and December are very good months for us, thank goodness."

She smiled a little then, and something warm began to unfurl in his chest.

No doubt about it, Haylie Smith was a damned

attractive woman. If she were anyone else, and they'd met any other way, he was pretty sure he'd have put the moves on her already. Offered to buy her a drink. Flashed his famed Trevor Jarrod playboy grin...the one that came complete with dimples and teeth so white and sparkly he could pose for a toothpaste ad.

But Haylie was off-limits, wasn't she? Not only because of the big, bad paternity issue she'd tossed on his doorstep with all the grace of a heavyweight fighter going down for the count, but because he got the distinct feeling she wasn't a woman who could be easily seduced.

Unlike her sister. Which brought him right back around again to the brick wall of the paternity thing.

"Ever planned a wedding?" he asked, returning to the kernel of an idea that had sprung up earlier.

Her brows knit a bit at that, but she answered readily enough. "A few. Small ones on my own, especially when I was first starting out. A couple of bigger ones once I'd hired staff to help out."

He hit the blinker, making a left turn that would take them farther from Jarrod Ridge, not closer, and hoped she was distracted enough not to notice. "They're a lot of work, I take it."

She chuckled. "Oh, yeah. Especially if you're dealing with a high-strung bride or family members who turn the entire event into a 'too many cooks' situation."

"But you enjoy them?" he pressed. "Wouldn't mind doing another?"

The lines crinkling her nose deepened, and her confused gaze completely focused on him now. "Of course not. It's Your Party, remember? No event too big, no party too small."

"Neither snow nor rain nor gloom of night..." he paraphrased with a teasing note.

"Exactly," she agreed with a laugh. "Although I do recommend event insurance if a client is putting a lot of money into something or the weather forecast is bleak."

"Smart move—if folks take your advice."

For a second, she didn't respond. Then her eyes narrowed and she said, "Why are you asking so many questions about my business?"

"Can't I just be curious?" he tossed back as he turned off the main road and onto a much more narrow private drive. Haylie was so engrossed in their conversation, she didn't seem to take note of the complete lack of traffic and the rougher drive as the Hummer navigated the snow-covered dirt-and-stone path.

Making a noise halfway between a scoff and a snort, she said, "Somehow I doubt you're ever 'just curious.'"

He grinned, thinking that even though they'd met for the first time only that morning, she knew him fairly well already.

"You're probably right about that. I've got a sister, though. Half sister, actually, who's engaged to be married. She and her fiancé were talking about a Christmas wedding, but they've put things off for so long and spent so much time waffling back and forth that I don't think they know what they want to do anymore."

They were climbing now, the oversize vehicle doing its job of hugging the road and navigating the less than smooth terrain.

"Where are we?" Haylie asked, finally realizing

that he hadn't driven them back to the resort as he'd promised.

Sidestepping the question, he told her instead, "So I was thinking that maybe you could talk with Erica. Maybe give her some pointers or help to allay her wedding jitters."

"I would be happy to. She can call me anytime, but..." Frowning, she twisted around in her seat just as his house came into view. "This isn't part of Jarrod Ridge. Is it? Where are we?" she asked again.

He remained silent until they reached the large two-car garage several yards from the main house. Both buildings were done in a dark, almost black wood stain that both stood out and blended beautifully with the rugged mountain terrain surrounding the property.

She was wrong about it not being part of Jarrod Ridge, though. No, it wasn't connected to the resort, but the small parcel of land he owned privately directly bordered the extensive Jarrod Ridge holdings.

Hitting the remote for one of the wide garage doors, he shifted to look at Haylie while the door slowly rolled upward.

"This is my place," he told her. "I thought I'd show you around, let you get a feel for the house before you turn me down flat on my invitation."

He could tell by the flattening of her lips and flare of her nostrils that she was *this close* to ripping him a new one. His only chance at avoiding a total nuclear meltdown was the hope that, with Bradley asleep in the backseat, she would be reluctant to wake him by launching into a full-blown tirade.

Trevor's eyes continued to blaze, and Haylie's jaw

worked as though she were grinding her teeth to keep from shrieking.

"Invitation?" she repeated, her tone acid sharp. "Don't you mean *order?*"

Five

"So that's it, isn't it. You're *ordering* us to stay here."

They were in the living room, logs crackling in the fireplace, the afternoon sun casting a lovely rose glow over the snowcapped evergreens and sleek white mountain slopes through the floor-to-ceiling windows that lined the west side of the house.

After taking a drowsy Bradley from his car seat, Trevor had given them a quick tour of the first floor while Haylie continued to fume. The baby was settled on a blanket in the middle of the floor now, his diaper changed and another bottle emptied. He was taking turns playing with his feet and a plastic ring of toys Haylie had pulled from her bag of tricks.

Haylie, however, was standing on the other side of the room, fuming. Her arms were crossed at her waist and her toe was tapping, actually tapping, in time with her bottled-up frustration.

"It's not an order," Trevor told her, doing his best to mollify her. Yes, he could force her to go along with what he wanted, but he would prefer to have her stay with him willingly. Or at least not as an adversary.

Moving into the open kitchen, he lifted two wineglasses from the rack hanging over the center island and pulled a bottle of his favorite merlot from the island itself. Then he went in search of a corkscrew.

"I'm *asking* you to stay here for a while," he continued, keeping his voice mild and hopefully cajoling without sounding patronizing. "So that I can be closer to Bradley. So I can get to know him through you, as well as getting to know you and learn more about your sister."

As well, keeping an eye on them. If they were under his roof, he could be sure she didn't do anything stupid like going to the press or deciding to seek her fifteen minutes of fame, along with a hefty payoff from the Jarrod family coffers.

With the cork free, he poured two healthy portions of the rich red wine and carried them back to the living area. He handed one to Haylie and was surprised when she took it—without tossing it in his face.

"If Bradley really does turn out to be my son, then I'd appreciate this time with him. Private time, before the rest of the world finds out that I fathered a son with a woman I don't remember, and then didn't find out about him for two months *after* her death."

Haylie cringed a bit at the word *death,* and he immediately regretted his matter-of-fact tone. Regardless of how he might feel about the woman who presumably kept his child from him for four months...and nine months before that, if he counted the full term of her pregnancy...he needed to remember she was Haylie's sister and that Haylie had loved her.

He took a sip of wine, pleased when she followed suit, then said in a softer voice, "You have no idea how callous the media can be when it comes to a family like mine. They keep us in the crosshairs of their telephoto lenses twenty-four seven, leaving us very little privacy, and turning every tiny occurrence into a major publicity campaign—to their benefit, not ours. They're especially talented at taking everyday, average events and blowing them completely out of proportion."

Tunneling his fingers through his hair, he blew out an aggravated breath. "If word were to get out about why you're here, even before we hear back from the doctor, headlines will be splashed across every gossip rag in the country labeling me a deadbeat dad and your sister a gold digger who intentionally got pregnant with a Jarrod heir."

Haylie seemed to consider that, swirling the merlot absently in her glass. Firelight reflected off the dark red wine and flickered shadows over her slim form while the muted sunlight shining through the window at her back cast her in an almost angelic glow that brought out the myriad shades of gold and brown and copper in her honey-blond hair.

His fingers itched suddenly to reach out and touch the silky strands, to find out if they truly were as soft and warm as they looked.

"Won't my staying with you, living under your roof, bring about a media frenzy just as much as if I were to go back to Denver and someone inadvertently found out about Bradley's parentage?" she asked.

Valid point. "We would keep that under wraps as much as possible, but if the question comes up, you're a family friend. That's all. A family friend and her son, staying with me rather than at the resort. We can even make it look as though you're a paying guest and I'm staying in the family quarters at the Manor so that you have this place all to yourself."

She cocked her head, looking skeptical, so he glossed over that sticking point and moved on to another of her bigger concerns.

"As for you taking time away from work, I don't know how long you took off after your sister's death, but surely folks would understand if you needed a bit more of a mourning period. And as I mentioned before, my sister really is in the process of planning her wedding. I'm sure she'd love having the help of a professional, and we can arrange it so that your stay here is actually a working visit."

Glancing down into her glass before lifting her gaze back to his, she murmured, "Are you sure your sister hasn't already hired a wedding planner? I mean, she is a Jarrod, after all, and can afford the very best. I would think hiring a professional is the first thing she'd think to do."

"I can't be sure, but I haven't heard anything about a wedding planner being hired, so I sort of doubt it." With a shrug, he drained the last of his wine and set the glass on the low, glass-top coffee table in front of the sofa. "If it makes you feel better, I'll call her right now."

Haylie opened her mouth to stop him, but he was already headed for the cordless on the kitchen counter.

To be honest, he hadn't intended to tell even his family about Haylie's sudden appearance and disturbing claims just yet, but he supposed they would find out soon enough, anyway. It wasn't as if he could take a few days off work or drag her to the Manor with him without the rest of the Jarrods swooping in to pepper him with questions. Sometimes, he thought wryly, they were worse than the press.

Hitting one of his many speed-dial numbers, he listened to the rings and waited for Erica to pick up. When she did, he greeted her with an upbeat, "Hey, sis, it's Trevor. I've got a question for you."

A second later, he shot Haylie an enthusiastic thumbs-up. "So how would you like to hire one? I'd consider it a personal favor, actually."

"Please tell me you aren't asking me to hire one of your temporary bimbos to plan my wedding," Erica begged with a groan.

Trevor didn't know whether to chuckle or be offended by her low opinion of his usual female companions. Not that he hadn't earned the reputation, he supposed.

But while it had never bothered him before, he found himself suffering a twinge. Of guilt? Embarrassment? He wasn't quite sure, but he didn't like the sensation.

Letting his gaze drift over Haylie's straight blond hair, conservative sweater and slacks, and classy but sensible shoes, he knew Erica would never mistake her for a bimbo. Or one of his temporary distractions, either.

"No," he answered firmly. "She's a very talented professional event planner, and I need to give her a really solid reason to stick around Jarrod Ridge for a couple of weeks."

"Why?" his sister asked without a hint of finesse.

"It's a long story," he muttered, looking down at the floor. "I'll explain later. So are you interested? Will you at least talk to her?"

"Of course. Frankly, it would be a relief to have

someone else worry about the details for a change. And someone to talk to about the wedding other than Christian. I love that man, but I swear he'd fly me to Galapagos if I asked him to, just to be married and done with it already."

"Great," Trevor responded, relief washing through him. "You two can arrange a face-to-face later, but for now, will you mind telling her that yourself?"

He held the phone out to Haylie and waited for her to take it. She did, reluctantly putting it to her ear.

"Hello?"

He couldn't hear the other side of the conversation, but Haylie nodded and offered his sister her name. For the next minute there were a lot of affirmative sounds and more nodding, followed by, "All right. I'd like that, thank you."

Hitting the disconnect button, Haylie handed the phone back to him. He knew her chat with his sister had gone well, but her expression was curiously blank.

"So?" he prompted, raising a brow.

"I'm apparently having lunch with your sister tomorrow to discuss the planning of her wedding."

"Excellent."

Haylie watched Trevor return the phone to its cradle, then collect the open bottle of wine and cross to the low coffee table where he poured a couple more inches for himself. Her glass was still nearly full, so he didn't offer to top her off.

Excellent? For him, maybe. She wasn't so sure about herself. She'd come to Aspen looking for a father for her nephew, not a new job.

Should she even help his sister with her wedding preparations, or should she back out of the impromptu lunch meeting she'd just agreed to? She could definitely develop a decent argument for temporary insanity, since not only her day but her entire life was beginning to feel very surreal and out of control.

On the other hand, they were talking about a Jarrod wedding here. *A Jarrod wedding!*

Celebrity-event planners would beg, borrow, steal and commit bloody murder to land a Jarrod wedding, and she was standing in the middle of Trevor Jarrod's living room being handed one on a silver platter. Even if they didn't pay her a dime, having a Jarrod wedding in her portfolio could take It's Your Party to a whole new level. From putting together mostly children's birthday parties and bar mitzvahs, to garden parties, high-society anniversaries and even more high-profile weddings.

The thought was so overwhelming that for a second she couldn't breathe, and the lack of oxygen caused tiny starbursts to flare in front of her eyes.

Forcing herself to take a deep breath before she did something truly embarrassing like fainting dead away while Trevor stood less than a yard from her, sipping his merlot, she reminded herself that she was projecting, blowing the entire situation way out of proportion. At the moment, the only thing her business future held was a harmless lunch date with Trevor's sister...and a decision to make.

Steeling her spine and her nerves, she fixed him with a firm glance and said, "I'll stay the night and meet with your sister tomorrow, but I'm not promising anything more than that."

"Fair enough," he agreed with the shrug of one shoulder. "Though I think once you talk to Erica, you'll decide that sticking around Jarrod Ridge for a couple of weeks isn't the worst idea in the world. And in case you're worried about losing profits while you're away from Denver, rest assured that we'll pay you well for your services. Very well," he added, winking at her over the rim of his wineglass.

Agreeing to stay overnight at Trevor Jarrod's house and actually following through were two entirely different things, Haylie soon learned.

For one, she had packed the car and made arrangements for a day trip, nothing more. She had enough formula and diapers for Bradley to get through the next few hours. If they were lucky.

For another, she had nothing with her *for her.* No nightgown or toothbrush or makeup remover, and only the clothes on her back to wear to her lunch with Erica the next day.

It was enough to make her reconsider her decision, that was for sure.

"Maybe this wasn't the best idea," she whispered, standing in the doorway of one of Trevor's extra bedrooms, staring at a comfortably snoozing Bradley.

He'd fallen asleep while finishing his bottle, and hadn't stirred while she'd changed him into one of the only remaining diapers. Of course, Trevor didn't have a crib or anything else that even remotely resembled a proper child-care necessity, so they'd had to improvise.

A soft, thick comforter on the floor in one corner, surrounded by pillows and a couple of the cushions from Trevor's expensive leather sofa, and she didn't think Bradley was going anywhere, even if he did wake up in the next few hours, which was highly unlikely.

"It's not that bad, is it?" Trevor asked from directly behind her. "I mean, it doesn't look great, but he's safe enough, right?"

Turning from the doorway, she nodded. "He'll be

fine. He doesn't move around much at all when he sleeps. The important thing is just to make sure he can't roll anywhere and that there's nothing nearby that will hurt him if he does wake up."

Leading her back down to the first floor of the elegant, expansive log cabin, he said, "Then why are you worried this wasn't a good idea?"

"Not Bradley, staying here. I wasn't planning to be gone overnight. I'm not prepared to stay *anywhere,* let alone with you."

Heat suffused her cheeks when she realized how that sounded, and she rushed on with her explanation in hopes that he wouldn't catch the slip.

"Bradley is almost out of diapers and formula, I have no personal items with me...." Slipping her hands into the front pockets of her slacks, she hunched her shoulders and looked down at her outfit. "Even if we get through the night, I'm going to end up looking like a bag lady when I meet your sister after having slept in my clothes and makeup."

One corner of Trevor's mouth tipped up in a grin. "You forget who you're talking to," he told her from across the kitchen island.

Sliding a pad and pen across the marble countertop, he said, "Write down everything you need. Be as detailed as possible—brand names, quantities, your clothing and shoe sizes. I'll have it all delivered tonight, along with your car."

"My car?" She tipped her head, watching his brown eyes and handsome face carefully. "Are you sure you want to have it brought here? Aren't you afraid I'll sneak off in the middle of the night with Bradley?"

"There may be exigent circumstances connected to your visit, but you're still a guest, not a prisoner. Besides, you gave me your word you'd stay through tomorrow, and I believe you."

"Why?" she wondered aloud. "You don't even know me." And she might very well be the gold digger she knew he suspected she was.

With a shrug, he said, "I think any woman who would take a day out of her life and drive four hours to tell me I have a child I knew nothing about—allegedly, anyway—just because she feels it's the right thing to do can be taken at her word."

Tossing back the last sip of his merlot, he set the glass down with a tiny clink before adding, "And you know what they say about keeping your friends close and your enemies closer."

Six

The next morning, Bradley had Haylie out of bed early, but he didn't wake her. She was already awake, having tossed and turned half the night before giving up on sleep altogether to simply lie there, letting her thoughts and anxieties run rampant.

Now, fresh from the shower and staring at the collection of clothing and accessories that littered the guest-room mattress, she decided that if this was an example of how Trevor treated his enemies, Haylie was sincerely considering becoming his nearest and dearest friend.

True to *his* word, not long after nightfall the evening before, a Jarrod Ridge employee had come to the door with everything from her list and more.

By the time the young man left, every inch of the marble island had been covered with fabric totes, a boxed dinner for two from one of the Ridge's exclusive restaurants waited on the counter near the stove and her car was parked in the drive. Trevor had thanked him with a nod and what looked to be a fifty-dollar tip, something Haylie quickly pretended she hadn't seen.

She'd known the Jarrods had money, of course. Which was sort of like saying the Sahara desert had sand. They were, in a word, loaded.

Yes, she understood that. And if she hadn't before driving down from Denver, the sight of the Jarrod Ridge Resort certainly would have clued her in. Trevor's demeanor of entitlement and the lavishness of his own private home were really just icing on the cake.

And though she considered herself a generous person, always tipping well at restaurants and after hotel stays, she didn't have a fifty-dollar bill in her wallet for emergencies, let alone floating around as extra change to give to a complete stranger in thanks for doing her a favor.

He hadn't been stingy when it came to supplying her with personal and baby items or a fresh outfit for her lunch with his sister, either. The vanity in the guest bathroom and the kitchen countertops all resembled a well-stocked drugstore, and the guest bed looked like the fitting-room floor of a woman trying to find the perfect dress for her high school reunion.

A new sweater and another pair of slacks would have been fine, but Trevor had apparently requested one of everything in her size from several of the resort boutiques. There were dresses and skirts and pants, blouses and pullovers and casual tops with both short and long sleeves. Even shoes and undergarments.

She couldn't decide whether to be impressed in a *Pretty Woman* sort of way or intimidated by the power Trevor so obviously wielded. He snapped his fingers and people jumped. He said, "Jump," and people asked, "How high?"

If the blood tests came back showing Bradley was his son—and she had no doubt they would, unless Heather had lied to her for the last year of her life—and Trevor got it into his head to fight for custody, she wouldn't stand a chance.

Haylie's heart seized in her chest at the thought, and her hands actually shook while she rushed to get dressed. She might not have money or power or even the biological rights that Trevor did, but she would still do whatever she had to in order to keep Bradley in her life.

She hadn't given it a lot of thought before making the trek to Aspen—something she was beginning to regret—but she realized now that it wouldn't be feasible for her to maintain full custody once the DNA results came in. The knowledge did nothing to loosen the low-level panic gripping her chest. But she would do anything and everything she could to make sure she was able to see the baby and spend time with him on a regular basis.

Surely Trevor would be open to visitation, right? He might be a Jarrod, used to getting his own way and ordering people around like pawns on a chessboard, but he wasn't cruel, was he? He wouldn't invoke his parental rights and cut her out of Bradley's life altogether. Would he?

Haylie wasn't sure what the symptoms of a full-blown panic attack felt like, but if her shallow breathing, sweaty palms and the ringing in her ears were any indication, she suspected she might be headed in that direction.

She needed to calm down. The test results wouldn't be in for weeks yet, so it wasn't as though Trevor was going to snatch Bradley out of her arms and run off with him. Considering the fact that he hadn't even held the baby yet—voluntarily, at any rate—she thought he was probably hoping the tests would come back negative so he could wash his hands of the whole situation and return to his fun-loving, playboy lifestyle with barely a ripple.

In the meantime, however, she had a business lunch to get ready for. One she was unaccountably nervous about.

Almost as nervous as she was about finally poking her head out of the bedroom and once again coming face-to-face with her host.

It had taken every ounce of composure she possessed just to get through last evening. Especially after half the bags from Jarrod Ridge had been unpacked and he'd carried plates of food to the dining area and invited her to eat with him.

What she'd really wanted to do was race upstairs and lock herself into the guest bedroom with Bradley. Bury her head under the quilted satin duvet and not come out until morning.

Playing ostrich seemed like such a good idea compared to remaining in Trevor's presence. She hated to admit it—*really* hated to admit it—but he intimidated her. In addition to his significant wealth, his towering height, broad shoulders and movie-star good looks were more than a little overwhelming.

Oh, she hadn't been the least bit overwhelmed or intimidated when she'd stuffed Bradley in his car seat and headed for Aspen to confront the man who'd unwittingly impregnated her sister and left a child fatherless.

Nor had she felt so much as a twinge of nerves while

she'd stared down Trevor's overprotective secretary, demanding an appointment with him, or sat in his office waiting for him to arrive so she could toss the cold bucket of reality in his face.

She hadn't even been worried when he insisted they go for blood tests immediately, even though it meant getting into a car with a man she'd never met before and letting him drive away from a public place crowded with witnesses.

Not the smartest thing she'd ever done, admittedly, but none of that had caused her a moment's hesitation.

Then somehow, somewhere along the way, the tables had turned and she'd gone from being a woman in control and on a mission, to a woman completely out of her element, maneuvered as easily as a remote-control airplane by her nephew's absentee father.

She felt completely at his mercy. Not only because she was staying under his roof, but because she knew how easy it would be for him to take Bradley from her if he really wanted to.

Which made her wonder if this luncheon with Trevor's sister was a good idea…or a mistake of epic proportions. Given how Haylie was feeling at the moment, she suspected it could go either way.

With a sigh, she took one last look around the room to be sure she had everything, then collected her purse and Bradley's diaper bag, and finally Bradley. The bedroom door swung open without a sound, and she moved just as quietly down the hall, down the stairs and into the main area of the house.

Trevor was already in the kitchen, awake and ready to start his day. Well, no surprise there, since it was past 10:00 a.m. He'd told her last night to take her time getting ready; that they would both go into the Manor just before she was supposed to meet Erica.

But unlike yesterday, he was quite obviously dressed for the office. Instead of a warm, thick sweater, comfortable jeans and Timberland boots, he wore a blue suit so dark it was nearly black, a bright red tie and dress shoes polished to a high shine.

She didn't know enough about designer clothes to properly place each item of his wardrobe, but she would have bet money none of them came off the rack, and that each bore some fancy, posh name like Gucci or Valentino or Armani.

Her own ensemble, provided by one of the exclusive Jarrod Ridge boutiques, had come with similar tags, but not by any designers she recognized. Just wearing them made her feel as though she was covered in something very fragile and valuable. Not the sort of clothes you wanted to snag or dirty or, God forbid, spill something on. And with a four-month-old whose favorite pastimes were chewing on her sleeve or spitting up on her shoulder, she was a walking bundle of nerves—for more reasons than one.

"Good morning," Trevor murmured as soon as he saw her.

He stepped forward, coffee cup in his hand, and she caught a sudden whiff of his cologne. Something crisp and clean and woodsy that reminded her of exactly where they were—a beautiful mountainside dotted with tall evergreens and sparkling with fresh snowfall.

She'd never before considered that the smell of trees could be sexy, but now the winter forest scent coming from the man in front of her had her knees going weak. His wavy, carefree hair, fresh-shaven face and Boss of the Year persona didn't hurt, either.

She swallowed hard, her grip on the baby tightening as her stomach did the slow roll of sexual attraction and…oh, so not good…longing.

"Coffee?" Trevor offered, completely unaware of the war currently being waged between her sensible mind and traitorous body.

She swallowed again, licking her dry lips before answering. "No, thank you."

She was already a writhing ball of anxiety, she didn't need to add caffeine to the mix.

With a nod, he finished the rest of his own coffee, then set his cup aside and headed for the door. Before she could pass through ahead of him, he slid both bags from her shoulder, leaving her with only Bradley to balance on her way to the garage.

When they arrived at his office, Trevor's secretary, Diana, was at her desk, as usual. And perched on the edge of that desk was a lovely, curvy woman. She wore a flowing, emerald-green blouse with tan pants, and her layered, silky brown hair just brushed her shoulders. The minute she saw them, she hopped to her espadrille-clad feet and smiled.

"Hi," she greeted them both. Then, bypassing Trevor, she held a hand out to Haylie. "You must be the wedding planner."

"Haylie Smith," she offered. "It's nice to meet you, Miss Jarrod."

"Actually, it's Prentice. I'm a newly discovered member of the Jarrod clan, but they love me, anyway. Right?" she said with a chuckle, slanting an amused glance in Trevor's direction.

"Do we have a choice?" he asked, deadpan. But while his face remained impassive, his brown eyes sparkled with affection.

Far from being offended, his sister grinned. "Nope."

Turning back to Haylie, she said, "But it doesn't matter, because you're going to call me Erica. And who is this adorable little guy?" she asked, zeroing in on Bradley.

Still bundled like a snowman at Haylie's hip, Bradley kicked his legs and giggled as Erica tickled one of his pudgy pink cheeks.

Clearing his throat, Trevor stepped forward and put a hand to the small of Haylie's back. The innocent touch shouldn't have sent currents of electricity rippling up and down her spine, but it did.

"Let's go into my office for a minute, shall we?" he murmured in a low voice, shooting his sister a meaningful glance.

Although her lungs didn't seem to be functioning properly in her chest and her feet felt like lead weights inside her shoes, Haylie managed to follow Trevor's prodding.

While he moved behind his desk and Erica took a seat in one of the guest chairs in front of it, Haylie went to the same sofa along the far wall that she'd used the day before. Laying Bradley on his back, she began stripping him of his snowsuit so he wouldn't get overheated now that they were indoors.

Leaning back in his chair, Trevor steepled his fingers and tapped them against his lips. "Normally, I'd prefer to keep this under wraps, but since it will probably come up during your lunch, and I don't want Haylie worrying about letting something slip, I think it's only fair that we tell you what's going on here."

Erica raised a brow, her gaze going from Trevor to Haylie and back again. "All right," she replied cautiously.

"And since you're my sister—a Jarrod now," he stressed, "I'll expect this to stay just between the three of us. We can't risk it getting out. The fallout would be astronomical."

His sister's mouth turned down in a frown. "You're starting to make me nervous. Just tell me already."

"There's a chance..." Glancing briefly at Haylie, who now had the baby balanced on her knees, he took a breath and gave voice to the words he hadn't even let himself truly consider yet. "There's a chance Bradley is my son."

For a second, his sister didn't respond. Then she blinked and did the owl thing again, looking from him to Haylie, him to Haylie...or possibly from him to the child on Haylie's lap.

"Oh, my goodness," she muttered, putting a hand to her heart.

"Yeah, I know," he agreed, wincing.

"You're my brother, and I love you, so forgive me for saying this, but..." She shook her head. "All that womanizing was bound to catch up with you eventually."

"I'm not a womanizer," he grumbled with a scowl.

Her eyes widened and she cocked her head to one side. "No, you're simply a connoisseur of the fairer sex and like to try a different flavor every week."

Which was merely a creative way of calling him a womanizer, he thought, his scowl deepening. But before he could argue the point further, Erica was out of her seat and crossing his office, making a beeline for the baby.

"You mean this might be my nephew? Why, he's just the cutest thing ever. May I?"

Haylie nodded and lifted the baby into Erica's waiting arms. "His name is Bradley."

"Hello, Bradley," Erica said in a high, baby-talk voice by way of introduction. "I'm your aunt Erica. Maybe."

Pushing to his feet, Trevor crossed to the two women, a frown still marring his brow.

"This is why I wanted you to know what's going on," he told his sister. Crossing his arms in front of his chest, he tapped the toe of one foot in irritation. "You can't let anyone hear you referring to him as your nephew. You can't link him to me or the rest of the Jarrod family at all, in any way, until we're sure."

Erica's head bobbed up and down in what could have been interpreted as a nod, but since she was busy cooing and laughing at Bradley, Trevor wasn't sure she was listening to a single word he had to say.

"This is important, Erica," he stressed in a firm voice, turning on his heel and beginning to pace. "We've already gone for blood tests, but the results won't be in for at least two weeks."

A dilemma his instincts were still screaming for him to throw money at. Cutting a generous check or paying for a new wing to be built at the local hospital had a way of speeding up test results, but that would only draw even more attention to a situation he was determined to keep strictly confidential.

"I've invited Haylie to stay with me until we find out for sure," he continued, uncrossing his arms from his chest and stuffing his hands into the pockets of his tailored slacks instead. "But she's concerned about being away from work for that long. She's a party planner, as you know, and has her own event firm in Denver. That's where you come in."

Stopping in front of his sister, he waited until she

met his gaze and he was sure he had her full attention. "I thought perhaps if we could *hire her* to plan an event for us, she wouldn't feel quite as uncomfortable about sticking around."

It was Haylie's turn to cross her arms. "I am in the room, you know," she chastised him. "And stop pressuring her. I won't have your sister or anyone else 'hiring me' for a job they don't need done just so you can keep me on a short leash until the tests come back."

Trevor opened his mouth, not sure whether he intended to apologize or strengthen his position and stand his ground, when Erica piped up.

"Actually, I'm glad you're here, Haylie. I really do have a wedding to plan, and just thinking about it is turning me into a nervous wreck. So let's go to lunch and have a nice, long chat, and if I end up hiring you, you can rest assured it will be because I want and *need* your help, not just because Trevor asked me to. Sound good?"

A beat passed while Haylie considered that. Then the tautness in her shoulders and spine seemed to wash away and she let her arms drop to her sides. Her gaze flicked to Trevor for a moment before settling back on Erica and Bradley.

"All right," she said softly.

Seven

As nervous as she'd been about going to lunch with Trevor's sister, Haylie couldn't believe how quickly the hours flew by. They'd talked about the weather, childhood memories and almost everything in between.

With a dreamy look in her eyes that told Haylie the woman was well and truly in love, while they'd picked at their salads Erica had shared the story of her whirlwind romance with her husband-to-be, Christian Hanford. She'd pulled a picture from her wallet of a very handsome, clean-cut, dark-haired man, showing it off in a manner that reminded Haylie of herself with pictures of baby Bradley.

As the Jarrod family attorney, the duty of telling Erica the truth about her parentage had fallen on Christian's shoulders after Donald Jarrod's death. Haylie couldn't imagine how shocking it must have been to have that sort of information dropped in her lap out of the blue.

To spend her entire life thinking one man was her father, only to be blindsided by the news that he wasn't, and that another man, now deceased, was.

Unless it felt a bit like having someone walk into your office and announce that you had a child you knew nothing about, she'd thought with a small sting of guilt.

And though she hadn't intended to spend any time at all talking about herself, before she'd even realized it, she was confiding in Erica about her rocky relationship with her sister. Their years growing up, when Heather had been the "pretty one," Haylie had been the "smart one" and it had seemed they were in constant competition—for their parents' affections, for attention, for friends and boyfriends.

She told Erica about her sister's apparent one-night stand with Trevor, and all the months that had followed leading up to Bradley's birth and Heather's tragic, unexpected death. And about Haylie's own almost pathological need to clean up after her sister, to try to do what was right one final time instead of what was easy and most often selfish.

By the time she'd finished, more than an hour had passed, and she was mortified at how much talking she'd done. How open and unguarded she'd been. She blamed it on the fact that she felt extremely comfortable in Erica's presence, as though they'd known each other all their lives.

Or rather, were becoming fast friends.

But while Haylie truly did like Erica, Haylie knew she couldn't get too close to the woman. For one thing, she was Trevor's sister, and Haylie wasn't even sure she would end up being friends with him, regardless of his biological ties to Bradley.

For another, Erica was about to become a client, and it was never smart to get too close or grow too comfortable with a client. Especially brides, since they had a tendency to be Pollyanna one minute and Bridezilla the next.

By the time they'd actually started to discuss potential wedding plans, their entrées were gone and they were sipping cups of strong, French roast coffee while waiting for dessert to arrive.

Even though she hadn't been at Jarrod Ridge long enough to try any of its other restaurants, Haylie had to admit that the Sky Lounge had been an excellent choice. And if this was merely a lounge, more of a bar with a limited menu, then the rest of the eateries the resort had to offer must be truly extraordinary. Of course, the fact that she was dining with one of the Jarrods probably had something to do with the level of service and amount of privacy they received.

After sharing more about their personal lives than either of them were probably used to revealing, and then finally getting down to the more vital topic of wedding plans, she returned to Trevor's office.

Erica was beside Haylie, having offered to walk with her so they could continue to chat. First, though, they'd had to retrieve Bradley from the colorful, bustling day-care center on the premises.

Haylie had balked at leaving the baby with anyone, especially out of her sight while she was technically in enemy territory. But Erica had assured her that they employed some of the best child-care providers in the state. Once Haylie had seen the facility and met some of the ladies watching over children of all ages, she'd decided turning Bradley over to someone else for a few short hours while she had a professional, adult conversation with Trevor's sister wasn't the worst idea in the world.

From there, the two women had strolled back to the main hotel and to Trevor's office. Haylie still couldn't believe how amazing Jarrod Ridge was. The more she saw of it, the more impressed she was by the many narrow streets and buildings of all shapes and sizes.

The main hotel—also known as the Manor—was the largest and the most important focal point of the resort. Apparently because—according to Erica's thirty-second recap of the Ridge's history—it was the first structure built by Trevor's great-great-great grandfather, and the rest of the resort had grown up around it. There were now private bungalows and shops and myriad activities available to keep visitors entertained.

Skiing was of course the main draw, at least during the winter months. But not everyone who vacationed at a ski resort was interested in actually hitting the slopes, so the Ridge also boasted a world-renowned spa, an ice skating rink, a bowling alley and an arcade for both the young and young at heart. The four restaurants spread throughout the resort served everything from quick deli sandwiches to fine dining and specialty cuisines.

It was like a tiny, self-contained village with everything guests could possibly want or need to make their stays more enjoyable. Even Haylie, who was here for reasons other than taking a holiday, was beginning to feel quite pampered and catered to.

As they entered the reception area of Trevor's office, Diana lifted her head and said, "You can go right in. He's expecting you."

Pausing in front of the double oak doors, Erica gave her a quick hug, Bradley and all. "Thank you so much for all your wonderful advice. I can't wait to tell

Christian that I'm not going to be such a raving lunatic about the wedding from now on. He'll be extremely grateful, believe me. He may even send you flowers," she added with a chuckle.

"I'm happy I can help," Haylie told her.

"You have all my numbers, right? And my email? And Christian's email, just in case?"

"Absolutely." Haylie tapped the side of her handbag. "My cell is loaded and ready to go. I'll be in touch soon."

"Excellent." With a wide smile, Erica leaned in and gave her another appreciative squeeze before spinning away and sauntering off.

As soon as she left, Haylie tapped on Trevor's door in warning, then let herself in. Turning from his computer, he leaned forward, resting his joined hands in the center of his desk.

"How did it go?" he asked.

She couldn't decide if he looked concerned or simply curious. Stepping forward, she lowered herself onto one of the guest chairs with Bradley on her lap.

"Fine. Well, even."

"Where did you eat?" he wanted to know.

"Sky Lounge. It was lovely."

The rooftop bar and sometimes grill had leather chairs and floor-to-ceiling windows that looked out over the sprawling resort, snow-covered mountains and miles of clear blue sky. She could only imagine how beautiful the view must be at night, all sparkling lights and black, star-filled sky.

Trevor inclined his head. "Good choice. It's a little less crowded up there during the day, especially at this time of year."

She nodded. "Except for a couple of people at the bar, we were the only ones there."

For several long minutes, the room was quiet, neither of them speaking. Then with a sigh, Trevor pushed back from his desk and stood.

"Why don't we head back to the house."

Haylie's eyes widened in surprise. "Can you do that? I mean, it's only three o'clock. Don't you need to stay until the end of the day?"

She wasn't sure exactly how she'd anticipated spending the rest of the afternoon now that her lunch with Erica was over, but she certainly hadn't expected Trevor to drop everything just to keep her company.

He flashed her a cocky grin that had her stomach doing somersaults.

"I can do whatever I want, I'm the boss. Well, one of the bosses, anyway. And while you were visiting with my sister, I made arrangements to be away from the office more than I'm here for a while."

Turning away from her, he began tossing files and papers into what looked like an expensive leather briefcase, standing open on a credenza beside the fireplace. "I can do a lot of work from home, and this way my schedule will be more open to spend time with you and Bradley."

For a second, she didn't say anything. She licked her lips, trying to get her racing pulse under control.

His offer made her uncomfortable, but she wasn't entirely sure why. Was it because she was coming to realize that she found Trevor attractive on more than simply the level of "gee, that guy's kind of hot"? Or because she was going to be spending *a lot* more time with him in the very near future than she'd originally intended?

"You didn't need to do that," she told him quietly.

With a shrug of one broad shoulder, he rounded the corner of his desk, coming to stand beside her. Or loom over, to be more accurate.

"It's done. Now let's go. You can fill me in on the details of your luncheon with Erica while I cook dinner."

She leaned back, her eyes once again going wide. "You cook?"

"I'm just full of surprises today, aren't I?" He flashed her that same cocky, amused grin before leaning over to pick up her purse and the diaper bag, adding them to the hand that held his briefcase. With a quick flick of his opposite wrist, he gestured for her to follow him to the door.

"Actually, I don't cook very often," he admitted as they crossed the office, "but I can hold my own with a pot of boiling water and a spatula."

At the door, he stopped and turned back to her.

"Tell me one thing before we leave," he murmured in a low voice.

Her chest tightened at the intensity in his dark-chocolate eyes and she swallowed in an attempt to dislodge the sudden lump growing at the base of her throat. When the lump didn't budge, she forced her chin down in a jerky nod.

"Are you sticking around for a while to help Erica with her wedding, or do I need to pack a bag and follow you back to Denver?"

She could tell by his expression that he found the latter option about as appealing as a full body wax—but that he would do it if that's what it took to keep her and Bradley close until the DNA results came in.

She still wasn't sure it was the smartest thing to do,

but at some point during her lunch with his sister, she'd made up her mind. Or perhaps had simply given up on trying to fight the innate stubbornness and determination that apparently ran in the Jarrod family.

"Erica wants a small, intimate Christmas Eve wedding right here at Jarrod Ridge, which only gives us a few weeks to pull everything together."

"So you'll stay?"

Please, God, don't make me regret this, she thought, even as a tiny voice in the back of her head ran through a laundry list of doubts.

"I'll stay."

A few hours later, Trevor carried two plates of pasta from the kitchen to the dining room. Rather than putting them at opposite ends of the long table, he'd created two place settings much closer together, at one corner. He told himself it was because Haylie hadn't yet filled him in on the details of her lunch meeting with Erica, and he didn't want to miss a word. But that wasn't entirely true, was it?

No, the truth was that Haylie smelled really good. Like citrus with a hint of wildflower. He'd noticed it when she'd first come downstairs that morning and he'd leaned in close to take her purse and the baby's diaper bag on their way out to the garage. It had stuck with him during the whole ride to the Ridge and seemed to fill his office long after she and Erica had left for their luncheon. It was as though the scent, her own unique fragrance, had crawled under his skin and taken root.

So, yes, he wanted to hear what she and his sister had talked about, reassure himself that she really would be sticking around until those test results came in. But he also found himself simply wanting to be closer to her. To that citrus-floral scent…to the silky blond hair that ran down her back and brushed the swells of her breasts… to the sparkle in her blue eyes and the lift of her rosy pink lips when she smiled.

Returning to the kitchen, he grabbed a bottle of wine and two glasses, letting his gaze trail to the stairs. She was up there now, giving Bradley a bath.

As soon as they'd gotten home, he'd changed from his suit into more comfortable jeans and a lightweight sweater, with the intention of impressing her with his culinary skills. Granted, they were limited, but he'd found that even the simple acts of boiling pasta and opening a jar of marinara sauce could be impressive to women as long as he did them with flair.

Unfortunately, instead of perching on a stool at the island to watch him work, the way his female guests had in the past, Haylie had decided to spend the last couple of hours upstairs with Bradley, feeding him, changing him and now getting him ready for bed.

Trevor suspected she was trying to avoid being alone with him, but that wouldn't last much longer. If she didn't come down on her own in the next thirty seconds, he fully intended to go up after her—and drag her to dinner, if he had to.

He was pouring the wine, hoping she would arrive before the pasta got cold, when he heard her padded footsteps on the stairwell. Tipping his head in that direction, he watched her take the last few steps and felt something strange tickle behind his rib cage.

She'd changed out of her blouse and slacks and was now wearing a pair of skintight black leggings with an equally snug short-sleeved top. The soft pink shirt had a faded floral design on the front, interspersed with tiny glittering rhinestones. She was wearing matching pink ballet flats on her feet and had pulled her hair back into a ponytail.

"Good timing," he said as she moved closer, rubbing the palms of her hands against her thighs nervously. He pulled out a chair and held it for her before taking his own.

"Did Bradley go down okay?"

She nodded, reaching for her glass of Barbaresco and taking a small sip. "I think being around all those other children at the day-care center wore him out."

"Is that a good thing or a bad thing?"

"Anytime a four-month-old child is happy or sleeping, it's a good thing, pretty much regardless of what made him that way."

Trevor chuckled, offering her some salad and fresh-grated Parmesan. "I'll remember that."

Shifting in her seat, she picked up her fork and started toying with the long strands of pasta on her plate, pointedly *not* meeting his gaze. "You didn't need to buy the crib and changing table and everything, though. We aren't going to be here that long and could have made do with just a bassinet or maybe a small playpen."

While they'd been gone that afternoon, he'd had the entire house fitted for Bradley and baby proofed. He hadn't known exactly what was needed, but thankfully there were professionals he could hire who did.

"Don't be silly," he told her, digging into his own meal. "You're a guest, and should have what you need to be comfortable. Besides, a baby shouldn't be sleeping on a pile of blankets on the floor, and if Bradley really is my son, then I'll be needing everything here, anyway."

The plastic locks on the cupboards and the playpen in the center of the living room were going to take some getting used to, and considering that Bradley wasn't even crawling yet, a lot of the precautionary measures leaned toward overkill. But just like the furniture, if Bradley was his, it would all be necessary eventually.

"Well, thank you," Haylie said quietly. "This is delicious, by the way."

"I'm sure your lunch at Sky Lounge was much better, but it's passable. And I'll tell you a secret." He paused, sipping his light red wine until she looked in his direction. "The sauce came from Emilio's."

"Really?"

"Mmm-hmm. If you like Italian, it is *the* place to eat at the Ridge—or in all of Aspen, frankly. The food there is much better than anything I could pull off, believe me," he offered with a self-deprecating wink. "If you like French cuisine, though, you really should try the main restaurant, Chagall's. I'll have to take you there sometime."

"I thought you didn't want anyone to know about our visit until you're sure about Bradley," she reminded him, taking a bite and chewing slowly. "Especially your family."

"Well, you've already met Guy. And I have a feeling Erica will make sure the rest of the family all knows that you're here and why. She'll swear them to secrecy, and they'll respect our privacy, but I wouldn't be surprised if several of them make up excuses to drop by over the next few days to check out you and Bradley."

"I'll keep that in mind."

"Speaking of Erica," he said between bites, "you haven't told me yet what the two of you discussed at lunch."

Tilting her head, her ponytail swung behind her. Her long lashes fluttered as she lowered her gaze. "It was just boring girl talk. Why do you want to know?"

"Call me curious. I feel a bit like a matchmaker waiting to hear how a blind date turned out. I'm the one who set the two of you up, now I want to make sure everything went okay."

Raising those cornflower-blue eyes back to his, her tone tightened. "I already told you I'd stay, if that's what you're worried about."

"I'm not worried." His teeth made a tiny clinking noise against his fork as he bit down harder than he'd intended.

He wasn't used to having to work this hard to get information. With women, he usually just smiled at them, maybe brushed his fingertips down the side of their arm, and they became either flustered enough or enamored enough to open their mouths and tell him anything he wanted to know. With men, a stern glance and subtle reminder of exactly who he was and of his family name had them delivering whatever he needed.

Haylie was different, though. She was a woman, so he suspected she was naturally attracted to him on some feminine level; they all were. But she was also stubborn and determined, which meant she wasn't going to let her hormones override her common sense.

And even though she'd agreed to his bargain of sticking around for the DNA results, he knew she wasn't entirely pleased about the decision. Something he couldn't blame her for, he supposed. After all, he got to stay right where he was, in his own home, working in his own office. She, however, had to adapt to a new environment, moving in with a man she'd just met, taking time away from her business and her friends and everything she was used to.

The complete upheaval of her life couldn't be easy

for her. Which was why he was determined to see that her stay remained as painless as possible.

Picking up his wineglass, he brought it to his lips. "I do want to be sure you and Erica are both content with whatever decisions you made, though. She's my sister, and I love her. I don't want her to feel pressured into working with you if the two of you didn't hit it off. And although I realize there are probably a hundred other things you'd rather do than stay here with me—"

"A thousand," she cut in shamelessly.

One corner of his mouth twitched. "A thousand others, then. I want to make sure you'll be at least relatively happy during your visit."

A few seconds ticked by while she seemed to consider that. He sipped his wine, watching as she twirled her fork over and over again through the long strands of pasta still on her plate.

"I like your sister very much," she finally replied. "And I think she must have liked me, as well as my ideas for her wedding, because she…"

She trailed off, her voice going soft, her head bowed.

"She hired you, I assume," he put in. "Otherwise, I doubt you would have agreed to stick around."

Dragging her gaze up to his, she nodded. And then she whispered, "She offered to pay me twice my usual rate."

She seemed embarrassed by the admission, though he couldn't fathom why.

"Excellent," he said. "You're worth it, I'm sure."

Haylie's brows drew together. "You can't know that. Neither can Erica. I could be the worst event planner in the world, ready to put her in orange taffeta and the groom in a powder-blue tuxedo."

He gave a low chuckle. "That would be quite the sight."

Shaking her head, she dropped her fork and leaned back in her chair, arms going across her chest in a clear sign of annoyance. "It's not funny. You're both putting an awful lot of faith in someone you don't even know. This is her *wedding,* for heaven's sake. One of the most important days of her life. She should be hiring someone she knows. Someone who's been recommended to her by all of her friends. Someone she has utter faith in."

Setting aside his own utensils, Trevor leaned back, mirroring her rigid posture. "First, I only asked Erica to meet with you, I didn't tie her up and order her to hire you—not that she would have, even if I had. And I trust my sister's judgment. If you hadn't impressed her with your knowledge and ideas while the two of you were together, she wouldn't have hired you."

Uncrossing his arms, he leaned forward, draping them on the edge of the table instead. "Second, she—and I, and the rest of the family—can afford to be generous with you. Erica could hire an army of stylists, if she wanted to, but I think the notion of a smaller wedding appeals to her, as does fewer people to help her organize the event."

Lowering his voice, he moved in even closer, making sure she understood the importance of his next words and just how serious he was about them. "Third, I want you here. You and Bradley both. If Erica hadn't hired you to plan her wedding, I'd have found another reason for you to stay. Believe me, Haylie, when it comes to you and that baby sleeping upstairs, money is the least of my concerns. I'll pay you triple, even quadruple your usual rate, if that's what it takes to keep you here until I can be sure I'm Bradley's father."

Eight

Haylie sat, stunned. The silence filling the dining room, and in fact the entire house, was thick and heavy, making her feel as though she'd been physically battered by Trevor's words.

She might not be comfortable with the situation, or thrilled with the way he'd maneuvered her into moving in with him, but one thing she could no longer doubt was his determination to see this through.

It impressed her, actually, as painful as that was to admit. Most men would be doing everything they could think of to avoid laying claim to some random woman's child, scrambling for excuses *not* to take a blood test.

But Trevor had not only insisted on a paternity test first thing, he wanted to keep Bradley under close watch until the results came in and he could know for sure that he was—or was not—Bradley's father.

Not only that, but Trevor was willing to take her in,

too, as the child's aunt, guardian and the closest thing Bradley had to a mother. Take them in, transform his house from a luxurious bachelor pad to one step up from a day-care center, and manufacture a job for her out of thin air to keep her from losing business or income while she was away from home.

Granted, she didn't *need* any of those things. She had her own apartment back in Denver, as well as a successful business. But the fact that he was willing to move heaven and earth to ensure their presence over the next couple of weeks raised her opinion of Trevor by several notches, at least.

Forcing herself to loosen her rigid posture, Haylie let her arms fall to her lap and gave a soft sigh. She preferred to categorize it as a tired sigh, not a defeated one, but there was a small part of her that had decided to wave the white flag of surrender.

She'd come here to let Trevor know about his son. It wasn't her fault that things had snowballed in a manner she hadn't anticipated, but since she'd already agreed to help Erica plan her wedding, already agreed to move into Trevor's house…was there really any point in battling over the fine points now? Wasn't it better to simply relax and let the unstoppable tide that was Trevor Jarrod sweep her away?

She gave a mental wince at that thought. All right, perhaps not entirely. She was too darned stubborn herself to simply roll over and let another human being dictate her actions or her life.

But a little acquiescence wouldn't kill her. And, in fact, if she gave Trevor's sister the wedding of her dreams, it might even prove quite beneficial to her livelihood down the road.

With that in mind, she picked up her fork, keeping

her attention on her plate as she said, "Erica told me that she and her fiancé had originally planned a big, summer wedding. But they've been so busy, and things have gotten so out of control that now they just want to be married already, without all the hoopla of a large reception."

Her willingness to talk seemed to relax Trevor as well. Sitting back in his chair, he reached for his glass, taking a drink of wine before returning to his meal.

"I'm not sure exactly how it came about, but she loves the idea of a Christmas Eve wedding. Something private and low-key, held at the resort, though we haven't decided yet on exactly where."

Trevor nodded, swallowing a bite of pasta before replying, "She'll have plenty of choices. We tend to have a nice handful of guests over the holidays, but aren't as full as usual. It shouldn't be hard to reserve a ballroom or two and keep most of the public from even knowing what's going on until after the fact."

"That's what Erica said. Pulling something like this together in only two weeks' time won't be easy, though. I'm going to need a place to work. A telephone, fax machine… It would really help to have my laptop and Rolodex," she murmured distractedly as an unending list of necessities and to-dos started scrolling through her head.

"Whatever you need. You can use my office here at the house, if you'd like, or we'll set up another room for you. I'll even run you back to Denver to collect some of your things," he told her. Then added with a wink, "As long as you promise not to abandon ship."

The wink sent her heart rate skittering, effectively hitting the brakes on the runaway train of her work-related thoughts. Seconds ticked by while her mind went blank and her temperature climbed degree by slow degree into the red.

What had they been talking about? Oh, right, a wedding. His sister's wedding. All the plans she had to put in motion in the rush to get everything done by December twenty-fourth.

Needing something to cool her down and hopefully get her brain cells functioning again, she tossed back the last few swallows of wine in her glass. It didn't help. What she needed was water. Ice-cold water, preferably in bucket form, being tossed right in her face.

Before she could even finish that nice little cooling-off fantasy, however, Trevor was stretching an arm in front of her to refill her glass with the lovely, brick-red liquid. As tempting as it was, Haylie refrained from emptying that glass, too, instead keeping one hand on her utensils and the other tucked away beneath the table.

Clearing her throat, she hoped her voice wouldn't squeak when she tried to speak. "Would you mind if I used the resort's child-care facility for Bradley? Not all the time...I don't like to be away from him for long stretches."

Even back home, she kept him with her at work and only left him with someone else for a few hours if she absolutely had to. Jittery brides tended to get annoyed with wedding planners who spend half their time bouncing and burping a fussy baby.

"But I know I'll need to do some running around, and also some touring of the Jarrod Ridge property, so it would probably be better to have someone else watching him then."

"Of course," Trevor readily agreed. Finished with his dinner, he crossed his legs and leaned back in his chair, the picture of quiet ease. "In fact, let me be very clear—you've got carte blanche while you're here, Haylie. Anything you need, it's yours."

Uncrossing his legs, he pushed away from the table and stood, collecting their empty plates. Gathering the cutlery and glasses, she followed him through the house to the kitchen.

"I'll see that you're set up with a winter-safe vehicle and a place to work, both here and at the Manor," he continued. "I can even arrange for you to have as many assistants as you'd like from the temp agency we use for the Ridge, and you can come to me or Diana for anything else you might need."

She helped him load the dishwasher, then leaned back against one of the counters to study him. It felt odd to her to see a man like Trevor doing such mundane chores. She would have expected him to have a cook and housekeeper, to be catered to rather than catering to her.

And he did exude that air of power and privilege at times. Especially when he wore a suit and tie and looked like he should be posing for the cover of *Forbes* or *GQ*.

The very thought made her knees go weak, and she dug her nails into the edge of the countertop to keep from sliding to the floor in a heap.

Oh, yes. He was handsome enough and impressive enough to make James Bond look like a vagrant. But he also possessed a very wide independent streak. She'd recognized that the minute he'd brought her to his house.

No family mausoleum or giant mansion with round-the-clock servants to satisfy his every whim. And though she was sure he had someone come in to clean at least once a week and could have anything he desired delivered within hours at the snap of his fingers, it was obvious he valued his privacy.

Probably because he liked to bring women home with him, and live-in staff would have cramped his style.

Her mouth twisted. That thought didn't sit very well. And then it twisted even more because she shouldn't have cared one way or another who he brought home or what he did with them once they were here.

But, oh, how she hated picturing him here with other women. In this same room, this same house... and upstairs in his bedroom.

She'd only gotten a glimpse of it during his initial tour, but she could well imagine the feel of those soft, hunter-green sheets beneath her bare skin. His hard, muscled body above her as they stretched out on the wide, king-size bed. His mouth and his hands and...

A wave of longing swept through her, followed by a blast of warmth that lit her up like a Christmas candle, she was sure. She swallowed hard and tried not to look conspicuously aroused as Trevor finished what he was doing and turned back to face her.

"Maybe you could even let me watch him some of the time."

Haylie blinked, praying he wouldn't notice the blush tingeing her cheeks, or the fact that she was panting ever so slightly.

God, she was such a sap. She should be keeping him at arm's length. Two or three arms' lengths. Not daydreaming about how amazing he probably looked without clothes on.

Shaking her head, she tried to clear the haze of lust fogging her brain and focus on his words.

"I'm sorry, what?"

"I said maybe I can keep Bradley once in a while when you're busy with Erica or whatever. It will give us a chance to get to know each other—man to man."

He offered a lopsided smile that had her heart flip-flopping inside her chest.

"Are you sure that's a good idea?" she asked with a mental wince. "Babies are a lot of work."

Instead of backing down, his expression hardened. "According to you, Bradley is my son. Which means I might as well start learning the ropes now."

Dark eyes flashing, he stalked toward her, closing the distance between them and making her shrink back.

Placing his hands against the marble countertop on either side of her waist, he leaned in, crowding her. She fought the urge to squirm as his warm breath danced across her face and his chest brushed the tips of her breasts. They might both be fully clothed, but she felt the touch right down to her soul, her nipples budding inside the cups of her bra.

"And I thought you could teach me what I need to know," he whispered, his gaze locked on her lips. "In the evenings, when you're not busy with plans for Erica."

She opened her mouth, wanting to tell him that in order to be ready for a Christmas Eve wedding, she would likely be working mornings, evenings and every minute in between. Sleep would be a luxury, never mind taking the time to give him child-care lessons.

But having him close enough that she could see the gold flecks in his chocolate-brown eyes and smell his cologne like it was a part of herself sent logical thought flying right out the window.

"All right," she agreed, almost as though someone else were speaking for her.

His head dipped in what she thought was a nod, and

FREE Merchandise is 'in the Cards' for you!

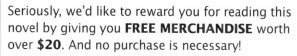

Dear Reader,

We're giving away FREE MERCHANDISE!

Seriously, we'd like to reward you for reading this novel by giving you **FREE MERCHANDISE** worth over **$20**. And no purchase is necessary!

You see the Jack of Hearts sticker above? Paste that sticker in the box on the Free Merchandise Voucher inside. Return the Voucher promptly...and we'll send you valuable Free Merchandise!

Thanks again for reading one of our novels—and enjoy your Free Merchandise with our compliments!

Pam Powers

Pam Powers

P.S. Look inside to see what Free Merchandise is **"in the cards"** for you!

(S-D-12/10)

W e'd like to send you two free books to introduce you to the Silhouette Desire® series. These books are worth over $10, but they are yours to keep absolutely FREE! We'll even send you 2 wonderful surprise gifts. You can't lose!

REMEMBER: Your Free Merchandise, consisting of **2 Free Books** and **2 Free Gifts**, is worth over $20.00! No purchase is necessary, so please send for your Free Merchandise today.

Plus TWO FREE GIFTS!
We'll also send you two wonderful FREE GIFTS (worth about $10), in addition to your 2 Free Silhouette Desire® books!

Order online at:
www.ReaderService.com

YOUR FREE MERCHANDISE INCLUDES...

2 FREE Silhouette Desire® Books

AND 2 FREE Mystery Gifts

FREE MERCHANDISE VOUCHER

2 FREE BOOKS and 2 FREE GIFTS

Please send my Free Merchandise, consisting of
2 Free Books and **2 Free Mystery Gifts**.
I understand that I am under no obligation to buy
anything, as explained on the back of this card.

*About how many NEW paperback fiction books
have you purchased in the past 3 months?*

☐ 0-2   ☐ 3-6   ☐ 7 or more
E9FY   E9GC   E9GN

225/326 SDL

Please Print

FIRST NAME

LAST NAME

ADDRESS

APT.#   CITY

STATE/PROV.   ZIP/POSTAL CODE

NO PURCHASE NECESSARY!

The Reader Service - Here's how it works:

Accepting your 2 free books and 2 free mystery gifts (gifts valued at approximately $10.00) places you under no obligation to buy anything. You may keep the books and gifts and return the shipping statement marked "cancel." If you do not cancel, about a month later we'll send you 6 additional books and bill you just $4.05 each in the U.S. or $4.74 each in Canada. That's a savings of 15% off the cover price. It's quite a bargain! Shipping and handling is just 50¢ per book.* You may cancel at any time, but if you choose to continue, every month we'll send you 6 more books, which you may either purchase at the discount price or return to us and cancel your subscription.

*Terms and prices subject to change without notice. Prices do not include applicable taxes. Sales tax applicable in N.Y. Canadian residents will be charged applicable taxes. Offer not valid in Quebec. All orders subject to approval. Books received may not be as shown. Credit or debit balances in a customer's account(s) may be offset by any other outstanding balance owed by or to the customer. Please allow 4 to 6 weeks for delivery. Offer available while quantities last.

▲ If offer card is missing write to: The Reader Service, P.O. Box 1867, Buffalo, NY 14240-1867 or visit www.ReaderService.com ▲

BUSINESS REPLY MAIL
FIRST-CLASS MAIL   PERMIT NO. 717   BUFFALO, NY

POSTAGE WILL BE PAID BY ADDRESSEE

THE READER SERVICE
PO BOX 1867
BUFFALO NY 14240-9952

NO POSTAGE
NECESSARY
IF MAILED
IN THE
UNITED STATES

then he lifted his gaze to hers. The heat and intensity there made her want to rear back...but she couldn't seem to move.

"I'm going to kiss you now, Haylie Smith," he murmured in a low, mesmerizing voice.

"Why?"

He grinned. "Because I've been thinking about it all night. I want to feel your lips, know what you taste like."

Oh, he should write greeting cards. His assertion melted her insides until she could barely hold herself upright.

She knew she should say no, push him away, but darned if her body would listen to reason. Instead, her lips parted and she whispered the only two words she could manage.

"All right."

Haylie's acquiescence was nice, but he didn't need it. At that moment, a herd of wild horses couldn't have stopped him from kissing her.

But even as Trevor covered Haylie's mouth with his own, he knew he shouldn't be doing this. The obstacles between them were enough to add an extra mile or two to the Great Wall of China. He couldn't have picked a more complicated woman to be attracted to if he'd walked into a psychiatric ward and announced he would pay a million dollars for a willing bride.

She was practically a stranger. She'd shown up in his office with a baby she claimed was his—and her dead sister's, no less.

And that was just the tip of the iceberg. If Bradley really did turn out to be his, then there was the whole custody issue to deal with. Custody, and the fact that he didn't know the first thing about being a father.

Trevor would never be able to turn his back on his own child. Say *thanks for letting me know about my kid, but I'm not interested in being a dad* and be content with sending a support check every month to assuage his guilt.

But he knew, with every fiber of his being, that if he voiced his desire to keep Bradley and be a true father to the little boy, Haylie would fight him every step of the way. She was bonded to the baby like nothing he'd ever seen before. Of course, given what he knew about her sister, he had no doubt that Haylie had stepped in to mother Bradley from the moment he was born.

He admired the hell out of her for that. But it was definitely going to complicate matters if the tests came back positive and he asserted his parental rights.

And still he kissed her. A soft brushing of lips at first, followed by a firmer pressing.

She felt exactly as he'd imagined she would—like rose petals or plush velvet. And she tasted even better. Like the Barbaresco they'd had with dinner—spicy and tart, but with an extra-sweet tang that was uniquely her own.

Leaning in a few brief inches, he let his body rest against hers. From chest to thigh, they touched, heat swirling between them and sending their temperatures—or his, at any rate—skyrocketing.

He brought his hands up, cupping her face and deepening the kiss. Running his tongue along the seam of her mouth, he urged her to open for him. When she did, he delved in, groaning at the explosion of sensation that rocked him.

Why did this feel so good? So right?

Haylie was not the first pretty girl he'd ever kissed. Far from it; he'd been with dozens—dare he say hundreds?—of women.

She wasn't even his type. Oh, he liked blondes well enough—as well as brunettes, redheads and everything in between. But where he normally didn't give much thought to a woman's hair one way or another, he had to admit that *hers* was spectacular, all honey highlights, like a ray of sunshine trapped inside a glass jar.

She was tall enough, about five-five to his six foot two. Slightly shorter than his usual arm candy preferences, but the top of her head came to his chin, which he thought was pretty much perfect. He liked looking down at her, and the idea of having her fit against him just right when he tucked her close.

Her fuller, more rounded figure was also an unexpected turn-on. He was used to the stick-thin model sort…high heels, high hair and size-zero bodies squeezed into belts that doubled as dresses that barely covered their rear ends.

And always before, that had gotten his motor running. Or maybe he'd simply had it in his head that those were the type of women he was supposed to be with—super-photogenic party girls who enjoyed being seen with a Jarrod heir almost as much as they enjoyed actually being with him as a man.

But therein lay the difference: They were girls and Haylie was a woman.

Haylie possessed none of the qualities he normally looked for in the opposite sex, yet he loved the feel of her soft curves pressed against his harder frame. Loved the way she looked and smelled and let him ravish her mouth without pulling away.

Threading his fingers into the hair at the nape of

her neck, he let his other hand stroke down the side of her throat, the curve of her breast, her waist. Then he reached the hem of her shirt, tunneling beneath to touch warm, smooth skin. A low, primal groan rolled up from his diaphragm, and he leaned closer, deepening the kiss.

This wasn't what he'd intended when he'd first decided to taste her. He'd only wanted a tiny nibble, something to satisfy his curiosity and maybe put her a little off guard.

Instead, it felt as though a brushfire had broken out just under his skin. Pinpricks of heat and sensation that urged him to keep going.

Forget about the *just a taste* thing. Forget about a quick kiss to assuage his interest. He wanted to lift her onto the counter right then and there and have his way with her. Wanted to pick her up and carry her upstairs to his bedroom where he could undress her slowly, lay her out on the satin sheets covering his king-size mattress and explore every inch of her luscious body. Slowly.

He wondered what Haylie would think of the erotic images suddenly flitting through his mind. She certainly hadn't pulled away when he'd told her he was going to kiss her. And since she still wasn't resisting—was in fact kissing him back with a passion and fervor that had his blood heading due south at a rapid pace—he thought there was a chance she might be willing to act out a few of them.

A scratchy, whimpering sound reached his ears, and he wondered if it originated from his own throat or from hers. But when it came again, even more persistently and from across the room, he knew neither of them was the source of the strange noise. Something else was.

When Haylie cocked her head and pulled away, he

knew he was right. He also had the satisfaction of seeing that her eyes were glazed and she was breathing hard.

A second later, before he had time to really enjoy it, she whispered "Bradley," and slipped past him before he had a chance to react. He watched in confused silence as she darted out of the kitchen and up the stairs, belatedly realizing that the scratchy whimper that had interrupted one of the best kisses of his life had come from the baby monitor in the living room.

Trevor couldn't say he was thrilled with this turn of events, but in an odd way, he was amused. Having the four-month-old ruin a perfectly good kiss that may very well have led to even more intimacies was his very first experience with fatherhood. And if Bradley turned out to be his son, it was something he should probably get used to.

Nine

The week and a half following "The Kiss," as Haylie had come to think of it, was a busy one. Partly because she really did have a million and one things to do to keep up with Erica's wedding plans, and partly because she was actively avoiding Trevor.

Unfortunately, making a point to avoid him physically didn't mean she could do the same mentally.

For some strange reason, he seemed to be deeply embedded in her brain. Whether she was on the phone ordering flowers and linens, or running around the Ridge trying to organize people and plans and locations, there was always a moment when his face or voice or the memory of his seductive cologne would pop into her head.

She blamed it on "The Kiss." Before that, she might have found him attractive, but not distracting.

The Kiss... Boy, howdy, had anything ever curled her toes like that before?

Sure, she'd been feeling mellow from the delicious meal he'd prepared for her and the exceptional bottle of wine they'd shared. And she could admit to more than a bit of curiosity, too. He'd told her in that low, mesmerizing voice of his that he was going to kiss her, and her inner fairy-tale princess had gone aflutter, thinking, "Yes, please." After all, one little kiss had never hurt anybody.

But that kiss had been about as far from a fairy tale as one could get. Oh, no. Fairy tales were sweet and soft and romantic, while what she'd experienced at Trevor's hands had been closer to a scene from a disaster movie. Oceans churning, volcanoes erupting, palm trees being whipped to and fro under gale-force winds.

The minute his lips had touched hers, the world as she knew it had ceased to exist. If it hadn't been for Bradley's sleepy whimpers echoing from the baby monitor, and the well-honed maternal instincts she'd developed over the past months that wouldn't allow her to ignore his needs, she would probably still be propped up against the kitchen counter, wearing Trevor like a warm fleece blanket. Letting him kiss her stupid...and oh, so much more.

She was very much afraid that if the opportunity presented itself again, they wouldn't stop at just a kiss, which was why she was determined to keep her distance.

In the mornings, she made sure to be dressed and ready and to have Bradley with her from the time she left the guest room, because she knew Trevor wouldn't make a move while she had the baby in her arms.

During the day, she stayed busy, busy, busy, whether she was working from Trevor's home office—which he'd generously let her take over—or running errands both around the resort and in downtown Aspen.

Evenings, though…those were tough. Even if all she wanted to do was put Bradley down for the night, then soak for a couple hours in a hot bubble bath, or fix a nice dinner for one and put her feet up while she watched a bit of TV, more often than not she found herself taking food to her room and hiding out there until she was sure Trevor had gone to bed.

Though the house was large and spacious, there was too much danger of running into him, too much chance of dim lighting and sleepy brain cells telling her it wasn't a bad idea to kiss him again, after all. Kiss him and touch him and let him take her to his bed.

Oh, no. She most definitely had to stay away from Trevor Jarrod. Although she was starting to understand how her sister had fallen for him so quickly. They might have shared only a less-than-memorable—at least on his part—one-night stand, but Haylie could see how his handsome features and charming personality would sweep any woman off her feet.

Pushing through the front door, she kicked it closed behind her, juggling the baby and her bags until she could unload some of them. It had been another busy day, but thanks to the Ridge's day-care center and the completely over-the-top, champagne-colored four-wheel-drive Cadillac Escalade Trevor had gotten for her to tool around in, things were going very smoothly indeed.

The first time she'd been behind the wheel, she'd felt completely ridiculous. It was like driving a tractor trailer. And she knew how much something like that cost—more than she could afford, and more than someone like Trevor should be spending on someone like her.

But as usual, he'd been resolute. Hidden the keys to her car, she suspected, since she hadn't been able to find them since the Escalade had been delivered. And she had to admit, it was a nice ride. Comfortable and much safer than her little sedan, she supposed, for both Bradley and herself.

So with Erica's help, she had menus completed for both the rehearsal dinner and wedding reception… rooms reserved…flowers ordered…linens, silverware, and glassware lined up… Invitations had gone out the week before to the small group of guests Erica and Christian had decided to include in their special day— mostly family and a few close friends—and RSVPs were already flooding in.

All in all, she was very proud of the progress they'd made in such a short amount of time. Of course, she suspected that as soon as the happy couple left the reception for their honeymoon, she would crash and burn, sleeping for a month straight.

In fact, just last week, when Erica has insisted she take an afternoon to relax and enjoy a full spa day with her, she'd fallen asleep on the table during her massage. Erica and Trevor's sister Melissa, as well as their brothers' significant others, Sabrina, Samantha and Avery, had all joined them. It had been a Girls' Day of sorts, something Haylie didn't get to experience very often given her hectic schedule and, yes, lack of close female friends back in Denver.

The women had kept up a constant stream of chatter and laughter, and though she'd managed to stay awake during their manicures, pedicures and cucumber face wraps, Haylie had simply drifted off during the massage.

Not surprising, considering how amazingly relaxing it had been, but still.

She had to admit that it had been both fun and informative to meet so many other members of the Jarrod clan. In addition to being gracious and friendly, they'd treated her just like "one of the girls," and she'd genuinely enjoyed herself.

As curious as she knew they must be about her sudden appearance in Aspen and her living arrangements with Trevor, they hadn't asked a single awkward question or given her even one piece of unsolicited advice about Erica's wedding. Something she had definitely been on guard about from the very beginning.

Dropping some of her things near the oak-and-marble island with a tired sigh, she started to shrug out of her heavy winter coat while simultaneously loosening Bradley's warm snowsuit.

"Hey."

Trevor's low voice startled her, and she jerked around to find him coming down the stairs. As usual when at home, he was dressed in jeans and a thick sweater. Today's choice was khaki-green and did amazing things for both his chest and eyes.

Not that she had any business noticing the mouth-watering appeal of either.

"Hi," she greeted him, still tugging and unzipping.

Moving through the house's open-design living area, he crossed to the kitchen and took Bradley right out of her arms. "Here, let me."

For a second, she froze, used to doing pretty much everything herself, and unused to having assistance with much of anything, especially the baby.

No, that wasn't quite true, was it? Ever since moving in with him, Trevor had been quite helpful. He'd supplied her with everything she'd needed to be comfortable and do her job for Erica, and then some. He was courteous and accommodating and was almost obsessively single-minded about lending a hand with Bradley.

As unnerving as it was on a lot of levels, he got definite brownie points for how involved he'd been in Bradley's care. He'd asked her early on to show him everything he needed to know about babies, adamant about learning how to prepare bottles and formula, change a diaper, give Bradley a bath.

He seemed to have a million questions—which was understandable, she supposed, from a man who didn't have much experience with young children, but suddenly found himself faced with the possibility of fatherhood. And more than once in the middle of the night, when she hadn't hopped out of bed quickly enough in response to Bradley's cries, Trevor had come to her door, tapping softly and offering to help with whatever the baby needed.

Given that they didn't even know for sure yet that Bradley *was* his son, he was certainly doing everything that could be expected of a new father.

On the one hand, having Trevor around to take care of everyday obligations that she was normally responsible for all on her own was nice. It relieved a modicum of her personal stress and gave her a little extra time each day to focus on the preparations for Erica's wedding.

On the other, she wasn't sure she liked somebody else playing parent to Bradley, even if that person most likely *was* his biological parent. But she was so used to caring for her infant nephew by herself, she didn't want anyone usurping that position, pushing her out of Bradley's life. And if someone else *could* care for him as well as she did, then that was a real possibility.

Oh, who was she kidding? When those DNA results came back and showed that Trevor was Bradley's father—which she fully believed would be the case—chances were he would take the baby away from her. Or try to, anyway.

Lord, why had she come here in the first place? It had seemed like the right thing to do at the time, but now… The thought of losing custody of Bradley made her blood go cold, and she wished she could go back in time and do the wrong thing by keeping the baby to herself.

Stripping Bradley down to his brown corduroy pants and long-sleeved duckie shirt, Trevor set the bulky snowsuit aside, then arranged the infant on his hip as if he'd been doing it half his life.

"Have you had dinner yet?" he asked.

She shook her head, still feeling slightly uneasy as she shrugged out of her own outerwear.

"You look tired. Why don't you go upstairs, change clothes, maybe take a long, hot bath. I'll get Bradley fed, and you can decide what you'd like to eat later."

It was as if he'd read her mind. She was tired and more than a little worn out simply from the schedule she'd been keeping lately, but while she knew she needed to eat at some point, what she *wanted* was to sink beneath about a foot of bubbles for an hour or two and let the hot water and steam-filled room wash away the stress and exhaustion of the day.

But she hated that he knew that…or could read her so easily. Or maybe she hated how reliant she'd become on him, knowing that he intended to take Bradley away from her once it was proven he was the baby's father—and how comfortable she was with that reliance.

The truth was, she *liked* living here, under Trevor's

roof. She liked coming home at the end of the day to find him here, or being here when he walked in the door. She liked talking to him, and looking at him, and smelling the faint scent of his cologne in a room long after he'd left it. And she liked having someone to help her with Bradley, to care *about* Bradley, after doing everything alone for so long and being the only person in her nephew's life who gave a damn about him.

But all of that also made her feel threatened, insecure. When it came to Bradley, the more Trevor learned to do on his own and the more confident he became in his ability to care for an infant, the less she would be needed. And when those tests finally came back, showing that he was the baby's father...well, she would be pretty much expendable, wouldn't she?

She pressed the heel of her hand to the center of her forehead, where a headache that hadn't been there five minutes ago began to pound right between her eyes.

"Go ahead," Trevor told her, moving around her statue-like form to the cupboard, where he began to collect assorted baby food jars for Bradley's dinner. "We'll be fine."

Yeah, that was the problem.

But without a word, she dragged herself upstairs, too tired and suddenly out of sorts to pass on the offer of a nice, hot bubble bath, even if it had been suggested by the man who'd put her out of sorts in the first place.

Resisting the urge to reach around and pat himself on the back, Trevor walked quietly into Haylie's room and laid Bradley down in the crib in the corner. He put the baby on his back, just as Haylie had instructed the first time she'd shown him how to put the boy down for a nap, and wound the timer on the jungle animals mobile hanging overhead.

He was pretty sure he'd remembered everything. After feeding Bradley, he'd given the baby a bath in his bathroom because Haylie was still locked in hers, then put him in a new diaper and Onesie. He'd even brought along a pacifier, which Bradley was busily sucking while his eyelids grew heavier and heavier.

Trevor was getting pretty good at this, if he did say so himself. As unhappy as he'd been when Haylie had first dropped Bradley in his lap, and as nervous as he'd been when he'd first decided to step up to the plate and learn his way around the care and feeding of an infant, he was now confident that if the paternity test came back naming him Bradley's biological father, he would be fully capable of caring for the child on his own. It would mean some rearranging of his life and normal routine, but he could do it.

Just as the baby's eyes drifted closed one last time and the suction on the pacifier slowed to only an occasional twitch of his soft, round cheeks, Trevor heard the bathroom door click open.

Raising his arms to the side like someone being held at gunpoint, he kept his back to that side of the room, hoping against hope that Haylie wouldn't be startled enough by his presence in her bedroom to shriek and wake the baby.

Not sure whether or not she'd noticed him yet, he took a step away from the crib and whispered, "Sorry. I was just putting Bradley down for the night."

He waited a beat, wondering if he was standing in the middle of an empty bedroom, talking to himself. But a second later, she whispered back.

"It's okay. You can turn around, I'm dressed."

Dressed, Trevor decided, when he'd done what she suggested, was a gross understatement.

Haylie stood just outside the bathroom in a pale peach robe that looked as if it was made of some kind of satin or silk that—unless his eyes were playing tricks on him—he could see straight through. At the very least, the diaphanous material was clinging to her damp skin in all the right places, making his mouth go bone dry and his groin tighten with want.

Her hair was twisted up and covered with a towel, but while he stood there trying to catch his breath, she tilted her head, swung her hair free and used the towel to continue to dry the long, damp strands.

He knew there was a four-month-old in the room with him, but all Trevor could think about was tossing Haylie down on the bed and making love to her. She was rosy-pink from her bath, some flowery fragrance wafting from the open doorway, and she was naked beneath that robe. It made him itchy, twitchy and hard.

"Did he get his dinner?" she asked, apparently heedless of the erotic thoughts racing through his brain.

He nodded, slipping his hands into his pockets to keep from doing something truly stupid like reaching for her, and rocking back on his heels. "And a bath and a fresh diaper."

Her eyes widened slightly and her movements slowed. She didn't say as much, but he knew she was surprised he'd managed so well all on his own. He half expected her to cross to the crib and double check that he hadn't taped Bradley's diaper on backward or stuck his head through the Onesie's leg hole.

He bit down on a grin when instead she only murmured a half-approving, "Good."

She twisted around to drape the wet towel over the bathroom doorknob, and her robe parted, the V at her neck opening just enough to flash the swell of one pale breast.

Sweat broke out along the nape of his neck and he could feel his flesh prickle as it grew taut around his muscles and bones. If he didn't get out of there soon, he was going to do something they would probably both regret, sleeping baby or no sleeping baby.

"I had the resort deliver dinner while you were in the tub," he said, because it was the first nonsexual thought that popped into his head. "There's a plate waiting for you downstairs. I'll heat it up while you get changed."

Without waiting for a response, he strode to the door and yanked it open harder than he'd intended. Once in the hall, he stood stock still, trying to catch his breath and regain his equilibrium.

Dammit, how could one woman shake him up so badly? He'd been with models, actresses, beauty queens... He'd dodged gold diggers and marriage-minded misses, extricated himself from women on the verge of becoming obsessive.

Then there was Haylie, who showed no interest in him whatsoever, asked nothing of him and maintained that she'd only sought him out in the first place to let him know he'd fathered a child.

Yet *she* was the woman that his libido apparently wanted more than any of the others. *She* was the one he couldn't stop thinking about, who kept him up nights for all the wrong reasons.

He'd kissed her once already, purely to satisfy his curiosity, but promised himself he wouldn't do it again.

Behind him, the door clicked, and he straightened,

feeling like a deer caught in headlights. He was supposed to be downstairs, busying himself as though he were completely unaffected by her presence. Instead, he'd gotten all of six inches from her room before overheating and stalling out.

Turning, he found her still in that sheer, lust-inducing robe and fisted his hands at his sides to keep from tearing it off her.

"I changed my mind," she said before lifting her head all the way. Before meeting his eyes. "I'm not hungry. I think I'll just go to bed."

With a curse, he reached around her, pulling the door closed, then backed her up against the hard, flat panel and boxed her in.

"To hell with it," he growled. "I changed my mind, too. I *am* going to kiss you again."

Ten

Trevor's mouth was warm and firm and just as spine-melting as the first time he'd kissed her.

Haylie knew, far in the back of her mind, that she should push him away. Kissing this man—or letting him kiss her, rather—was not a good idea. After the last time they'd done this, she'd made a long, long list of reasons why, mentally repeating them to herself often and sternly.

At the moment, however, she couldn't think of a single one. Not when only items from the "Pro" column seemed to be jumping up and making themselves known.

Like how the winter-fresh scent of his cologne wrapped around her, clinging to her nearly as tightly as his arms wrapped around her waist. Or how intoxicating his lips were. Both soft and unyielding, they brushed and pressed and nipped, commanding her to respond like to a snake charmer's flute.

Of their own volition, her arms lifted to circle his neck, and she leaned even more heavily against the closed door. Her legs were the consistency of rubber bands, only the door and Trevor keeping her upright.

A million reasons not to let this happen, and only one in favor of dropping her reservations and going with the tidal wave of passion threatening to bowl her over: She wanted him.

Pushing every other thought, every other caution aside, she let go and threw herself into the kiss. As though he sensed her capitulation, Trevor moved closer and deepened the pressure of his mouth. She moaned, tangling her tongue with his and threading her fingers into his hair.

When her leg came up to bracket his hip, her bare foot teasing the back of his knee, she knew she was in trouble…and knew he knew it, too.

Pulling his mouth from hers, Trevor rested his brow against hers, his chest rising and falling with his ragged breathing.

"Come to my room with me," he whispered, the pad of his thumb rubbing back and forth, back and forth across her cheek. "Let me take you to bed."

Could he possibly believe she was going to say no? After two of the most amazing kisses of her life and the way she was draped around him now, in the middle of the hall?

Of course, at this very second, she couldn't form much of a response either way. Words failed her because her lungs were still straining for oxygen, her throat still thick with longing.

So she nodded and tightened her leg where it wound around his hip, which she hoped was answer enough.

It was. Blowing out a pent-up breath, Trevor grabbed

her by the waist and lifted her, pulling her against his body. She brought her other leg up and crossed her ankles at the small of his back, meeting him halfway when he leaned in to kiss her again.

Then they were moving. Trevor spun to the left and stalked down the hall, carrying her as though she weighed no more than little Bradley.

With barely a pause, he pushed the door of his room open, then kicked it closed behind them with the heel of his foot. A moment later, she found herself falling backward, bouncing as she hit the firm king-size mattress.

Trevor followed her down, covering her with his long, hard body even as his hands began to explore her own. They slipped beneath her robe, touching her bare skin as he brushed the material away.

First he uncovered her thighs, taking the time to stroke them outside and in as he went. Then he moved past her hips to her waist, where he unknotted the robe's sash and spread the two sides apart to reveal her breasts and torso.

Swallowing hard, Haylie resisted the need to pull the robe back together or cover herself with her hands. Trevor was staring down at her like an explorer who'd just discovered the Lost World. It was both disconcerting and flattering—and the only thing that kept her from squirming under his blazing hot gaze.

She couldn't remember the last time a man had looked at her with such blatant intensity. Or the last time she'd wanted one to…or wanted one just as much.

Eyes twinkling, dark hair tousled and falling carelessly around his handsome face, Trevor lowered his head and kissed the hollow of her throat, then trailed his lips down the center of her chest. Between her breasts and over her stomach, his touch made her burn.

When he reached the apex of her thighs and placed his mouth right at the heart of her, she nearly shot off the bed. But Trevor was having none of that. He flattened one large, rough-palmed hand over her abdomen, holding her in place, while he shifted between her legs, parting them even farther and making himself comfortable.

She had to admit, this wasn't what she'd expected. From the minute she'd decided to throw caution to the wind, she'd expected something fast and furious. A flash fire of passion, scalding hot, but quickly burned to embers. And, yes, more than a bit of selfishness on Trevor's part.

He was a Jarrod, for heaven's sake. One of the Jarrod Ridge Jarrods of Aspen, Colorado. Rich beyond her wildest imaginings, able to buy and do whatever he liked. A man used to getting his way in all things. She knew *that* from personal experience.

She also knew from all the newspapers and magazines he'd appeared in over the years that he was used to dating extremely glamorous, extremely beautiful women. Two characteristics Haylie could never claim for herself.

Oh, she was attractive enough. Not movie-star gorgeous, but not in line at the grocery store for a bag to put over her head, either. Of course, the ten or fifteen pounds that made her a little more lush than society's image of womanly perfection would definitely push her to the other side of Trevor's penchant for chopstick-thin model types.

As far as being glamorous went... She was too busy building her business and taking care of Bradley to worry about keeping her hair flawlessly coifed or making sure to wear the latest designer fashions. Some days, she was lucky if she remembered to put in earrings or got her shoes on the right feet.

Yet here she was, sprawled naked on the bed of a man she was sure would never have looked twice at her if they hadn't been thrown together through bizarre circumstances, and he was being extremely...anything but selfish. Incredibly *un*selfish, in fact.

Her hands clawed at the quilted duvet as he increased the pressure of his mouth. When he hit a particularly sweet spot, she nearly shrieked, hips shooting off the bed. Trevor's hands flexed where they framed her thighs, and she could have sworn she felt him smile.

Smiling was the furthest thing from her mind, though. He was creating entirely too many amazing, mind-boggling sensations for Haylie to even form a coherent thought, let alone control her facial expressions.

All she knew was that her entire body was on fire. She was writhing, panting, straining for a completion only he could give her.

"Trevor, please." The words slipped out before she could stop them. She hated to sound so desperate, even though she was, and bit the inside of her lip to keep from saying anything more. Saying, moaning, begging...

Thankfully, he didn't make her speak. Kneading her thighs like a hungry kitten while she clutched at his thick, wavy hair, he redoubled his efforts, using his tongue and teeth to tease the tiny bundle of nerves hidden between her folds. Before she could manage a full inhalation of short, broken breaths, pleasure swamped her, hitting her like a bolt of lightning and sending her arching up from the mattress with a keening cry.

She hadn't quite come down to earth yet when Trevor slid up the length of her body. Her lashes fluttered as she opened her eyes. No easy feat.

This time, she did smile. A small, wavering smile, but a smile all the same.

He was naked. Deliciously so. Though she had no idea when he'd stripped out of his sweater and jeans. Had her eyes been closed for that long? Or had she actually lost consciousness there for a minute after that orgasm?

It had been an incredible orgasm, so her guess was loss of consciousness.

Returning her grin with a very self-satisfied one of his own, he lowered himself on his forearms, covering her from breast to ankle. The heat of his skin seeped into hers, warming her like a bonfire, and she took a deep breath to inhale his wonderful scent.

Against her better judgment, she lifted her arms and draped them around his neck. She was surprised, really, that she could move at all; her bones and muscles were the consistency of runny gravy.

"That was awfully nice of you," she murmured by way of a thank-you.

The corners of his mouth twitched. "Glad you liked it."

"'Like' *sooooo* doesn't cover it," she said with an unladylike snort.

If possible, his grin turned even cockier. She could practically feel his ego growing by leaps and bounds.

"I'm a gentleman," he told her, leaning in to nuzzle her throat. "And gentlemen always make sure ladies come first."

She chuckled, the sound weak and still slightly breathless. "I don't think that's how the saying is supposed to go."

"My bed, my rules."

"Really?" She tilted her head, giving him better

access. "Do those rules include pleasuring a woman so thoroughly, she falls asleep immediately afterward, leaving you to your own devices?"

He raised his head, brow arched. "Definitely not."

"Well, you're in trouble, then. Because that one did me in. I'm ready for a nap." Stretching her arms up over her head, she gave a wide, theatrical yawn.

"Hmm." The sound rolled up his throat, low and thoughtful. "Guess I'll just have to change your mind about that."

With an exaggerated sigh, she arched her back and let her eyes drift closed. "I suppose you can try."

Amusement flashed across his features while determination sparked in his espresso-dark eyes. "I do love a challenge."

Oh, so did she. But where this one was concerned, she didn't think she'd last very long.

Returning his mouth to the side of her neck, he kissed her pulse point, then let his tongue dart out to lick the spot, followed by gentle sucking. That alone sent her heart racing…a fact she was sure he could feel beneath his lips.

He kissed a trail up the line of her throat, over her jaw and to her mouth. That was when she discovered what a kiss really was. Not counting that first scorcher in the kitchen. Or the second scorcher outside her bedroom door.

When their lips met, it was as if all the oxygen had been sucked out of the room in one giant gulp. And when his tongue delved inside to tangle with hers, everything around them burst into flame.

Tiny explosions went off in her bloodstream, making her wrap both her arms and legs around him even more tightly. She stroked his hair, his shoulders, his back.

Moaned when he began to do the same at her breasts. Soon his mouth followed, licking, circling, gently suckling until her nipples were stiff, pebbled peaks, so sensitive, she could hardly stand it.

She'd known from the start that Trevor was a man used to getting his way, one who didn't like to lose. Now she also knew never to challenge him or doubt his determination. Because even though she'd only been teasing when she'd mentioned leaving him to his own devices, she was now very interested and very much involved, whether she liked it or not.

Which didn't mean she was going to let him be in control—at least not entirely. Working her hands between their bodies, she used her thumbs to toy with his own tiny, flat nipples...and earned herself a deep groan.

Given Trevor's love of outdoor sports and his level of activity, it shouldn't have surprised her that he had an amazing physique. But truly, she thought, he was *amazing*.

Almost everything about him was rock solid—biceps, pectorals, six-pack abs. He should be the poster boy for the local gym, or even for Jarrod Ridge.

Put a tanned, sweaty, half-naked Trevor on a few posters advertising the best skiing, rock climbing, white-water rafting in the state, and men and women alike would flock to Aspen in droves. The men in hopes of getting a bit of his adventurous streak to rub off, the women in hopes of tracking down Trevor and checking out all of those sinewy male muscles for themselves.

Yet for now, at least, they were all hers.

Letting her fingertips slide down the center of his chest, she stroked her way to another hard, impressive muscle. She brushed the backs of her knuckles up and down his velvety length, smiling when he released her mouth in order to draw in some much-needed air.

"You're killing me," he panted, a lock of dark hair falling forward over his brow.

"Not yet," she murmured in her best sultry, Marilyn Monroe voice, "but soon. If you're lucky."

He gave a breathy chuckle, then startled a small yip out of her when he rolled and shifted until he was sitting in the middle of the bed and she was perched above him, her bottom perched on his knees.

"Do your worst," he told her. "I can take it."

"Do you have a condom?"

Trevor stretched out an arm, patting the top of the comforter until he found the foil packet he'd dropped within reach earlier. Holding it between two fingers, he offered it to Haylie, a punch of longing slamming into his solar plexus when she took the square from him and tore it open with her teeth.

Oh, yeah. Taking her to bed was *definitely* one of his better ideas. Maybe not smart in the long run, but at the moment, he considered it freaking brilliant.

He sucked in a breath and clutched the bedspread in his fists to keep from shooting off like a rocket when she covered him with the thin layer of latex. She was barely touching him, and it certainly wasn't the first time a woman had put a condom on him, but for some reason, having Haylie do it—*watching* her do it—was one of the most erotic experiences of his life.

And if he survived the rest of the night—which, at this point, was doubtful, very doubtful—he swore to repay her for every little bit of torture she was doling out on him. What was good for the goose, tit for tat, and all that.

Once the protection was in place, Haylie lifted up

on her knees, hovering over him as she ran her fingers through his hair, tipped his head back and kissed him. Softly, sweetly, and arousing as hell. As though he needed any more fuel thrown on his fire.

While their mouths were still locked together, she reached between them to wrap a hand around his straining erection...a move that had him gripping her waist and thrusting his tongue even deeper. Positioning herself just right, she sank down, inch by agonizing inch, until she was fully seated, taking him to the hilt.

Sensation swamped him, and from the digging of her nails into the meat of his shoulders, he suspected she was feeling the same.

As promised, he let her set the pace. For several long minutes, all they did was kiss, which was just fine with him. He thought he could probably spend from now until eternity kissing this woman and never get bored. Her taste and texture were just too damn intoxicating.

When she was ready, though, she began to move. Carefully at first, lifting herself only an inch or two. Then sliding back down. Again and again until his teeth ached from the delicious friction and his muscles twitched from holding back.

Just as his already thready control was about to snap, she broke their kiss, gasping for air and arching so that her breasts were right in front of his face. And how could he resist such a delectable offering? Flicking his tongue over one raspberry tip, he urged her on, wanting to increase the burn of satisfaction for her the way she was for him.

He watched her cheeks flush and the pale curve of her lashes flutter as her eyes closed. His own eyes were wide open, and he intended to keep them that way. He wanted to see every shift of color across her skin, every hitch of her chest with her rapid breaths, every degree of pleasure that showed on her face.

And when she came again—very soon, if he had anything to say about it—he wanted to see that, too.

Wrapping his arms around her waist, he pulled her closer. Her breasts flattened against his chest, sweat-slick skin to sweat-slick skin. She rearranged her legs to circle his hips, ankles locking and riding the small of his back, and he let his hands float along the small indentation of her spine until his fingers could twist in her hair, bring her mouth closer to his own.

Lips and tongues met, twined, fought for dominance, while at the same time, their lower bodies moved in tandem. His back and forth, hers up and down, creating ripples of bone-melting sensation that brought them closer and closer to the edge.

And then they were over. Haylie gasped, shuddering and spasming around him. The feel of her body tightening, clenching on his rocked him to his core and straight to a climax of epic proportions.

Squeezing her hard enough to break something, he gave one more high, powerful thrust before his body stiffened and he spilled inside her.

Eleven

Hours later, Haylie shifted in her sleep, bobbing toward consciousness. She was warm and cozy and more comfortable than she could remember being in a long, long time.

And then she realized why. A heavy arm draped her waist, a heavy male body framing her from behind.

She was in Trevor's bed. In Trevor's arms.

A stab of something... Fear? Regret? Clutched her heart even as she admitted to herself that making love with him was one of, if not *the,* most amazing sexual experiences of her life. It complicated things, without a doubt, but it had also made her eyes roll back in her head.

Before she could decide whether to stay and drift back to sleep or extricate herself from Trevor's firm hold and sneak back to her own room, she heard a squeak.

Bradley. That must have been what had awakened her in the first place.

Doing her best not to wake Trevor, she lifted his arm from her waist and slowly rolled out of bed. Her robe was a mass of wrinkled material on the floor, where it had gotten tossed hours earlier, but she picked it up, shook it out to find which end was up, and quickly covered herself, tying the sash as she tiptoed out the door.

Her bare feet padded on the cool hardwood floor as she crossed the hall to her room. Inside, Bradley was lying on his back in the crib, face crinkled and arms and legs flailing as he fussed.

She scooped him up, patting his back as she carried him downstairs to the kitchen to fix a quick bottle. Taking the baby and the bottle back upstairs, while Bradley drank she sat in the beautiful, hand-carved rocking chair Trevor had insisted she have.

Once Bradley's belly was full and he'd fallen asleep again, she put him in a clean diaper and returned him to the crib, hopefully for the rest of the night. She didn't even know what time it was and had to check the clock when she returned the dirty bottle to the kitchen.

Five after two. She had to be up again in only four more hours. But the question now became, did she go to her room and spend those hours alone...or return to Trevor's bed and curl up next to his warm, firm body?

Oh, she so wanted to do the latter. The thought was almost irresistible. But that didn't mean it was smart. Sleeping with him once had been stupid enough; better not to compound that by making Bad Decision Number Two.

Rinsing the baby bottle, she left it in the sink to be dealt with in the morning, and turned to head back upstairs. A shadow fell across the tiled floor, rising over her and sending her back a step. She opened her mouth to scream, then quickly caught herself as her eyes adjusted and she realized she wasn't about to be swallowed whole by the abominable snow monster.

"Good lord," she breathed, slapping a hand over her chest to stop the rapid pounding of her heart, "you scared the life out of me."

Rather than offer an apology, Trevor's dark eyes blinked sleepily and he rubbed a hand through his tousled hair. He'd pulled on a pair of blue-and-white-striped flannel pajama bottoms, but both his feet and chest were still bare.

She'd never noticed before how sexy his feet were. Of course, the last time he'd been wearing so few clothes she hadn't exactly been interested in his toes.

"I woke up and you were gone," he said in a tired, gravelly voice.

"The baby woke me," she told him. Not that she owed him an explanation. If she'd been smart, she would have sneaked out of bed even without Bradley's prompting and locked herself in the guest room, well away from roving hands and tempting lips.

"Is he okay?"

She nodded. "Needed a bottle and a new diaper. He's back to sleep now."

Trevor tipped his head, which she took as a sign of approval. Then he took a step forward. And another. And another.

Haylie retreated, not sure what his intentions were, until the counter stopped her. But it didn't stop Trevor. He continued stalking her until his chest brushed the tips of her breasts. She wondered if he could feel her nipples budding through the thin satin of her robe.

"Trevor," she whispered as he leaned in, began nuzzling a spot just beneath her ear.

"Mmm-hmm."

"What happened before..." She trailed off. It was so hard to concentrate while he was doing that with his mouth.

"Mmm-hmm."

"It was..."

He licked the lobe of her ear, then nipped gently with his teeth, and her knees nearly buckled.

"A mistake," she forced out breathlessly. "It was a mistake."

"Definitely," he agreed, though the fact that he was now kissing a hot, wet path to the hollow of her throat made her think he didn't agree, not really. "A terrible mistake."

She swallowed, determined to keep her mind on track and *not* let him distract her, no matter how hard he was trying.

"Then why are you...doing this?"

His fingers slipped under the belt of her robe, untying the knot and letting the garment fall open. Cool air hit her overheated skin and she shivered.

"The way I see it," he murmured, sliding his hands inside her robe and pushing it open wider, "the mistake's already been made. Can't undo it."

He made a good point. Maybe only because his hands on her breasts and his mouth on her collarbone were as intoxicating as a bottle of fine wine, but still...

"We're both consenting adults," he continued, kissing a path down the center of her chest. "I don't see any reason why we shouldn't continue to enjoy one another for as long as you're here. No strings, no promises. Just—" his tongue darted out to sweep across one tight, sensitive nipple "—pleasure."

Her head fell back on a shudder, her eyes slipping

closed. He made another very good point. The man was clearly a genius, his skills obviously wasted at a menial marketing job for Jarrod Ridge when he could be curing dreaded diseases, negotiating world peace and discovering life forms on other planets.

A tiny voice sounded inside her head, a faraway echo offering a small semblance of sanity. It forced her to open her mouth and say, "But…"

That's all, just "but…" She knew there should be more, knew there was some kind of argument she should be posing, but darned if she could think of a single one.

So Trevor finished the thought for her. He straightened enough to reach her mouth, kissing her until the only thing taxing her brain was a flurry of stars in swirling colors.

He broke away, giving her a chance to catch her breath, but only for a second before grasping her waist and hoisting her onto the countertop.

"It's only for a week or so more," he told her, nudging the robe from her shoulders and letting it float down her arms to pool at her hips. "As soon as those test results come in, everything is going to change. But until then, we've got nothing but time."

He kissed the curve of her breast. "To spend together."

Her collarbone. "Alone."

The line of her jaw. "Just the two of us."

And finally, her mouth. "Enjoying ourselves—" his hands cupped her knees, prying her legs apart so that he could step closer and fill the space; the flannel of his pajama bottoms was soft and highly erotic against her inner thighs "—in increasingly pleasurable ways."

There was only one thing she could think to say to

that, while his lips ravished hers and his thumbs circled closer and closer to her center.

"Okay."

Two days later, Haylie returned from the Ridge earlier than usual. She shouldn't be doing this. She had a mile-long list of things to do, and contrary to her fondest wishes, the time leading up to Christmas Eve and Erica's wedding seemed to be speeding up rather than slowing down.

But Trevor had finally convinced her to let him take her to dinner at Chagall's. Even if they requested a private booth, tried to slip in under the radar, they were bound to be noticed. By the staff, by other guests, and eventually word would reach the kitchen. Trevor didn't seem to mind, so she was trying not to worry about it, either, but that didn't mean she was looking forward to being fodder for the Jarrod Ridge gossip mill.

Then again, maybe no one would even notice them. It was possible. It was also possible that Trevor had prepared for any such scrutiny and had a perfectly plausible story in mind to explain what the two of them were doing together.

The problem was that while they'd agreed to act as though they were merely business acquaintances and weren't on a date, a date was exactly what this evening's dinner would be. At least she assumed so, given the fact that she was living under Trevor's roof and currently sharing his bed.

She knew she should be feeling guilty about the last, but heaven forgive her, she didn't. Not yet, at any rate. And she promised herself that when the end came—which, of course, it would—she would handle it in a mature fashion. No tears or histrionics, because she and Trevor had agreed that there were no strings or expectations to this affair. They were simply two consenting adults enjoying each other's company for as long as it lasted.

But an affair, by definition, was supposed to be kept under wraps, wasn't it? Full of clandestine meetings and secret rendezvous. Not going out to a crowded restaurant in a very public resort where anyone could see them and speculate about their relationship, begin all manner of ugly rumors.

It was Trevor's call, though, and he'd insisted they do this now, before she got too much more swept up in Erica's wedding preparations. She suspected, too, that it had something to do with wanting her to experience the five-star opulence of Chagall's before those DNA test results came in.

Maybe he wanted to impress her. Though she didn't know how she could be any *more* impressed, given everything she'd already seen of both his personal home and the family's holdings.

Or maybe he was simply trying to be nice, to give her a bit of a break from all the hard work and long hours she'd been putting in on his sister's behalf. Of course, such a large job had been his idea in the first place, and his way of keeping her close until he found out Bradley's paternity.

But still, Trevor was being kind and romantic, and she was just weak enough to go along with it, to let herself be swept up in the fantasy, however short-lived it would turn out to be.

Bradley was still at the resort's day-care center, so she didn't need to worry about him. And she had a good hour to shower, change clothes and redo her hair and makeup before meeting Trevor back at the resort, at his office, as they'd agreed.

Kicking off her shoes just inside the door, she shook off her coat and hurried upstairs. Twenty minutes later, she hopped out of the shower and began the ritual of drying and styling her hair, applying a few dabs of her favorite perfume and touching up her makeup to something a bit heavier and more appropriate for evening than work.

From there, she walked barefoot to the guest-room closet and pulled out the little black dress she'd been thinking about all day. When she'd first noticed it among the wardrobe offerings Trevor had had supplied for her, she'd thought it was entirely too fancy for anything she'd be doing during her stay in Aspen.

But the moment he'd convinced her to dine with him at Chagall's, she'd known she would finally put the velvet sheath to good use. She'd also known exactly what shoes and jewelry she would wear with it—a pair of steep, nearly four-inch open-toe stilettos with tiny white bows on the sides and a triple strand of ivory pearls with matching earrings.

When she was pretty much ready, she grabbed a small black clutch large enough to hold a few necessary items such as her cell phone and lipstick, then realized she didn't have a watch. She must have left it in Trevor's bedroom.

She really tried not to leave her things in his room, because even though they were *technically* living together and *technically* now sharing a bed, moving anything into his room felt too personal, too much like true cohabitation or like this was all leading somewhere. But considering the number of times he'd lured her in there fully dressed, then stripped her down...a shiver

skated down her spine at the warm, intimate memories…
it was no wonder she'd managed to leave something
behind.

Crossing the hall, she pushed open his door and
moved toward the nightstand, where she most expected
her watch to be. Halfway there, she noticed a lump in
the center of Trevor's bed.

Odd, since she remembered straightening the
covers herself that very morning. She might not have
managed hospital corners or done as good a job as his
housekeeper, but she definitely hadn't left a big, messy
lump in the middle of the mattress.

It took a moment for her brain to process what she was
seeing, but then she started to wonder if something had
happened. She'd spoken to Trevor that morning before
they'd parted ways outside his office at the Manor, but
not since. There hadn't been a need, since their plans
for dinner had been ironed out the night before.

But what if he hadn't been feeling well? What if he'd
eaten some bad sushi for lunch or some such, and had
come home sick? She'd like to think he would have
called or texted her about that sort of thing, or even had
Diana contact her, but perhaps he'd been *too* sick even
for that.

Stepping forward, she reached for the covers, slowly
drawing them back as she whispered his name. "Trevor?
Are you all right?"

But it wasn't Trevor beneath the bunched up sheets.
At least not unless he'd grown three feet of extra hair
and dyed it a bright copper-red over the last six hours.

Dropping the covers like they were a nest of wriggling
vipers, she jerked back, eyes wide.

Behind her, she heard a creak and turned to find
Trevor waltzing through the open bedroom door. His

hair was still short and brown, and he was wearing the same suit he'd left the house in earlier that morning.

He grinned at her, sweeping up to press a quick, hard kiss to her lips. His hand at the base of her spine was firm and possessive, and even with the cold reality of what was lying in the bed beside them, it warmed her.

"I thought I'd pick you up for dinner instead of making you drive back to the Ridge by yourself. Besides, it's easier to drop off my briefcase now than remember to pick it up later on our way out."

Licking her lips and removing probably half of the lip gloss she'd just painstakingly applied, she did her best to find her voice.

"Really?" she asked. "You didn't come home early for a little afternoon delight?"

His grin turned into a full-blown leer. "I hadn't, but if you're offering..." He tipped his left wrist to check the time. "Our reservations aren't until seven, and one of the many perks of being a Jarrod *is* that we can be late and still get a table."

He leaned in, going for another kiss, but she quickly sidestepped, moving farther away from him. His hand dropped from her back and his smile slipped, sliding downward into the beginnings of a frown.

"What's wrong?" he asked, sounding genuinely concerned.

"I wasn't talking about me." She cocked her head toward the bed. "I meant Goldilocks over there."

His eyes darted to the lump under the covers that was just starting to wiggle around and wake up. In three long strides, he reached the bed and stretched out an arm to whip back the sheets and spread.

A long, lithe form with curly red hair and wearing only a matching hot-pink bra and high-cut underwear blinked thick lashes and rolled from her side to her back. Her lips curved when she spotted Trevor.

"Hi, baby. Hope you don't mind that I let myself in."

That was all Haylie needed to hear. Or maybe all she could stand to hear without becoming ill or violent, or both.

Spinning on her heel, she marched from the room. Of course, by the time she got downstairs, she wasn't sure what to do.

She could have stormed out, climbed back into the Escalade that didn't belong to her and drive away...but where would she go? Jarrod Ridge? Home to Denver? A local hotel? Any of those options would require returning to the resort to pick up Bradley, at the very least.

But deep down she knew she wasn't going to do any of those things. She also knew she didn't really have a right to be upset at all.

What business was it of hers if Trevor had another woman in his bed? If he had a dozen Playboy bunny girlfriends on the side?

She and Trevor might be sleeping together—a decision she'd known from the outset wasn't the wisest move of her life—but no one had ever said their relationship was an exclusive one. In fact, they hadn't called it a relationship at all.

And she'd known his reputation with women, known he had a girl in every port, so to speak. Could she even be surprised that one had popped up out of the blue? Although, it would have been nice if this particular flavor of the month hadn't popped up in his *bed* while Haylie was still sharing it with him, but that was the risk one ran, she supposed, when one chose to take up with Colorado's most notorious ladies' man.

Which meant Haylie needed to get over it. Stop acting like a jilted lover, a jealous spouse.

But just because logic was winning out over raw, knee-jerk emotion didn't mean she could shed the physical effects of her upset quite as easily. Her heels click-clacked on the polished hardwood floors as she stalked to the giant stone fireplace. It was cold now, empty, but she didn't care.

Crossing her arms beneath her breasts, she slowly began to pace. Not out of anger, exactly, but more to burn off the excess energy still thrumming through her bloodstream and give her something to do while she waited for…whatever she was waiting for.

Though she doubted she and Trevor would end up going to dinner now, she was overdressed for anything else. And even going back upstairs to hide in her room wasn't an option because she was too afraid of running into Trevor and his copper-haired bimbo along the way.

So she stayed where she was, wearing a path in front of the fireplace until she heard footsteps upstairs, moving closer. Bracing herself for what was to come, she dropped her arms and tried to look as casual and unruffled as possible.

The woman was fully dressed again, though parts of her silver lamé jumpsuit looked like it was painted on. Her hair was piled on top of her head like a giant, flame-red crown, and big, chunky jewelry graced her neck and wrists. Haylie was sure the outfit was the height of fashion, but she looked a bit like a stowaway from the disco era. Her makeup was also smudged in places, and every few steps she would sniff, then wipe at her nose as though she'd been crying.

Trevor, on the other hand, was the picture of stoicism as they made their way down the stairs, single file. He kept one hand on the railing, the other in his trouser pocket and his gaze firmly on Haylie.

Haylie watched them move through the house to the front door, watched the woman turn on her go-go booted toe to flash doe eyes at Trevor and run a manicured fingertip down the center of his chest over his navy-blue tie.

"Are you sure, Trev-Trev?" the redhead murmured in a clear pout. Her lips were pursed in a deep frown, her lashes batting fast enough to cause a draft.

To his credit, Trevor didn't respond to the woman's flirtations, except to grasp her hand and very firmly move it back to her side. "I'm sure. Have a safe flight, Isabelle."

With that, he opened the door and saw her out.

Haylie didn't want to believe that the woman's departure could affect her one way or another, but as soon as the door closed behind Isabelle with a click, a wave of relief washed over Haylie. But only because it meant there would be no ugly arguments, no petty confrontations. Right? Certainly not for any other reason.

Pushing away from the front door, Trevor started walking slowly in her direction.

"I'm sorry," he said. "That definitely wasn't how I intended this evening to begin."

"That's all right," Haylie responded, ever so proud that her voice came out steady and sure. "It's none of my business who you invite into your bed."

Okay, so that didn't sound quite as detached and aloof as she might have hoped.

Halting in front of her, he cocked his head, lifting a hand to the side of her face. "I didn't invite her," he said softly. "At least not recently. We dated a while back, and I guess she was hoping we could strike things up again."

"Since she had a key to your house, I guess she wasn't far off the mark."

His lips quirked up in an indulgent half smile, and Haylie locked her jaw, telling herself to keep her mouth shut before he started to take her comments as a sign of jealousy.

"She knows where I keep a spare, though I'm thinking I should probably change that now. And she only climbed into my bed to wait for me because she was tired. She's a model and just flew in from her last shoot in Paris."

A model. Of course. Haylie should have guessed as much from the woman's perfect body, perfect hair, and how perfect she'd looked standing next to Trevor, all tall and lovely and photo-ready.

Haylie's aversion must have shown on her face because Trevor gave a low chuckle and brushed his knuckles across the line of her jaw. "Don't worry, I sent her away. For good. She won't be bothering us again."

Haylie would have been lying if she hadn't felt a small thrill at his words. But the reality of the situation was close behind, reminding her that she didn't belong here, and that today's Sleeping Beauty was only the first in a long string of women Trevor had wrapped around his pinky and was dangling like marionettes from his fingertips.

Licking her lips, Haylie whispered, "There is no us. Not really."

Rather than draw away, as she'd expected, a tiny, bittersweet smile tugged at his lips. "At the moment, there is. And I'm not going to let a surprise visit from a presumptuous runway model ruin that *or* our plans for the evening. Now," he said in a firmer tone, retreating a step, "are you still interested in dinner at Chagall's or would you prefer to stay in?"

Haylie's first instinct was to say "neither." His uninvited guest had been like a splash of cold water, startling her out of her warm but misleading cocoon.

Even though she'd warned herself not to, she'd grown comfortable under Trevor's roof. Sharing his bed. Moving through his world as though she belonged there. Sticking her head in the sand and letting the fantasy of living in Aspen, with all that it encompassed, carry her away.

On the other hand, maybe Isabelle's impromptu arrival was exactly what Haylie needed to remind her *not* to get too comfortable with her current circumstances.

She couldn't leave, because she'd promised Trevor she would stick around until the paternity results came through. And by agreeing to arrange Erica's wedding, she'd sort of inadvertently agreed to stay through the Christmas holiday, hadn't she?

It certainly wouldn't do for the wedding planner to up and run off before the actual nuptials. Especially over something as unreasonable as discovering that her temporary (and accidental, really) lover had other girlfriends. Not when she'd known from the very beginning that he was the playboy type. How hypocritical it would be of her to get upset now simply because she'd been slapped in the face by the flesh-and-blood evidence of his true nature.

So she couldn't leave Aspen because she'd given her word, and she couldn't stomp off in a snit because she didn't have a right to *be* in a snit. And either way, Bradley still needed to be picked up from the resort's day-care center.

Taking a deep breath, Haylie forced her mouth to curve in a smile. And, really, it wasn't that difficult. Not once she'd put things into proper perspective.

Her current situation might not be ideal, not the fairy-tale romance she might have created for herself if she were the author of this story, but it was one she'd walked into with eyes at least moderately wide open. She'd made her bed, so to speak, and until he kicked her out of it or something more significant happened to change her mind, she was going to share that bed with Trevor.

Twelve

Haylie was unaccountably nervous. It was the Friday before Christmas Eve and a week before Erica and Christian's Christmas Eve wedding. But more importantly, it was Erica and Christian's rehearsal dinner, all planned and prepared by Haylie herself.

Which meant it needed to go off without a hitch. Not only because she wanted everything to be perfect for Erica, but also because she took immense pride in the events she organized.

But being in the same room with so many Jarrods was more nerve-racking than she'd anticipated. Especially considering her ongoing affair with Trevor.

Did they know? Had he told any of them, maybe let it slip? Had someone seen them standing a little too close? Speaking a bit too intimately? Acting too familiarly with one another?

What if they could tell, just by looking at Haylie, that

she spent her nights in his bed, making love with him in a thousand different ways? Wonderful, amazing ways. Ways that she was going to miss and long for once she left Aspen and went back to Denver.

Did her cheeks flush when she glanced in his direction? Did she stammer in response when someone asked her how she was enjoying her time at Jarrod Ridge?

Her only hope was that even though everyone in the room knew Trevor quite well, they didn't really know her, and would perhaps excuse any odd behavior on her part as the simple anxieties of an event planner coming up on *the* big event.

Although Trevor's brother Guy had volunteered chefs from the various restaurants to prepare the evening's meal, the dinner itself was being held on the Manor's rooftop, at the Sky Lounge, which they'd temporarily closed to guests.

Tables had been arranged and place settings laid out. Soft, romantic instrumental music filtered through the air, wine flowed liberally and members of both the family and wedding party had been mingling for the past half hour.

Haylie was pretty sure she'd met all of the Jarrods now, as well as their significant others. Erica, of course, she was starting to know rather well just from the amount of time they'd spent together the past few weeks. And she'd been introduced to most of the ladies during the spa day Erica had organized.

Now she was also becoming acquainted with more of the men. She'd interacted with Christian and Guy occasionally because of the wedding plans. Then there were Trevor's brothers Gavin and Blake, and Melissa's fiancé, Shane McDermott.

Thankfully, she was good with faces and names—it was sort of a necessity in her line of work—otherwise, she suspected it would have all been very confusing.

At a signal from the kitchen staff, she started strolling through the room, asking everyone to please make their way to the table, where dinner was about to be served. Normally, once that was done, she would quietly slip into the background again, keeping an eye on the party, but also coordinating with the kitchen to make sure everything was running smoothly.

Tonight, however, she was pulling double duty as both hostess and guest. At Erica's insistence that she join them, and Trevor's reassurance that her presence was more than welcome, there was a place set for her near the end of the long, cloth-draped table, directly on Trevor's left. This would allow her to be involved in the dinner party, but also to jump up and make a quick escape if she was needed elsewhere.

For the first time all evening, Haylie let herself take a deep breath and relax as napkins were placed on laps and the waitstaff began to serve the salad course. So far, the party had gone off without a hitch. Everyone seemed happy, and everything was going exactly as planned.

To her right, Trevor was dressed in a stylish, dark blue suit with a lighter blue tie that made him once again look as if he should be posing for the covers of magazines. Of course, that was true no matter what he wore—a business suit, jeans and sweater or worn flannel pajama bottoms.

Not when he was naked, though. When he was naked, she thought he could grace the cover of a much sexier, much more adult women's magazine. Just thinking about that—and accidentally letting herself picture him as she'd last seen him gloriously naked—made her breath catch in her lungs.

Since the night one of his model ex-girlfriends had decided to play Goldilocks by climbing into his bed uninvited, Haylie had done a much better job of compartmentalizing her responsibilities and her feelings. She'd let him take her to dinner at Chagall's, taken pleasure in the evening as though it were a real date, and put thoughts of all his other women out of her head.

Not the smartest choice, perhaps, but it was the one she'd made and the one she'd come to terms with. Despite the Goldilocks incident, Trevor had done nothing, said nothing, to make her think he was seeing another woman—or women—while she was sharing his bed and his home.

She had no illusions that she and Trevor had a future together, but she'd given herself permission to pretend, just for a little while, that the future didn't exist. To enjoy the short time she did have with him and push everything else away.

Call it denial. Call it delusional. She preferred to think of it as walking on the wild side for once in her otherwise very prim and proper life.

Heather had always been the carefree one in their family. The happy-go-lucky risk taker, while Haylie was the careful, staid sister. Heather had gone through men like cold sufferers go through tissues. Haylie had dated maybe ten different men in her entire adult life... and some of those had been one-time encounters over nothing more than coffee.

Trevor was like her get-out-of-jail free card. Letting herself get involved with him wasn't smart, it wasn't practical...but it *was* going to be a memory she pulled out on all of those cold, lonely, dateless winter nights to come.

So she was going to enjoy him, dammit. Without feeling guilty, without second-guessing herself. And hopefully, when the fantasy came to a screeching halt, she wouldn't end up too damaged, either physically or emotionally.

Beside her, Trevor smiled and reached beneath the table to pat her knee. Which would have been fine, except he left his hand there, his thumb gently rubbing her stocking-clad thigh.

So much for relaxing. His touch made her the very opposite of relaxed, causing all of her nerve endings to buzz like live wires.

If they weren't careful, someone was going to notice that something was going on between them. Or more to the point, if *she* wasn't careful. Trevor was completely calm, completely unruffled, looking no different than at any other time, while she felt as though her face was a kaleidoscope of emotions for the whole world to see.

She was so wrapped up in the uneven beat of her heart and the pounding of her pulse in her veins that she missed the first several minutes of conversation at the table. It wasn't until she heard the word *wedding* that her brain kicked in and began functioning properly, reminding her that she was on the clock and needed to be awake and alert to her clients every whim.

Whoever had mentioned the wedding, though, wasn't talking about Christian and Erica's upcoming nuptials. They were grilling Trevor's brother Guy and his fiancée, Avery, about their plans. From what Haylie gathered, the two of them had been involved for quite some time, and the family was beginning to wonder why they hadn't tied the knot yet. Or perhaps pressuring them to get the show on the road already.

Across from her, Haylie noticed a rosy flush climbing toward Avery's hairline.

"Actually, we haven't gotten around to making any wedding plans yet," Guy responded in a low tone, pointedly taking Avery's hand and twining his fingers with hers on the table between them. "And...well, we've been keeping it under wraps, but now that we've discovered we're expecting, we may have to put it off a while longer."

It took a brief second for Guy's words to sink in, a moment in which the entire lounge was eerily silent, given the number of people occupying the room. But a second after that, chaos erupted. Cheers and high-pitched feminine shrieks of joy mixed together as several family members rose from their chairs and circled the table to surround the happy couple, offering hugs and hearty handshakes.

Haylie stayed in her seat, part of the dinner party, but not really part of the family revelry. Once everyone had returned to their spots, she offered her congratulations and said, "If there's anything I can do to help with the wedding plans—when you *are* ready to plan something, that is—I hope you'll let me know."

"Oh, that would be wonderful." Avery breathed in what could only be described as acute relief, lifting her free hand to her chest. "I have to admit, I really would like to be married before this pregnancy becomes too obvious, but the whole idea is so overwhelming, I don't even know where to begin."

"I felt the same way," Erica put in from her place beside Christian at the head of the table. "But Haylie is amazing. She thought of everything, and then took care of it all before I even had a chance to get stressed. It's been so nice to be able to sit back and relax, letting someone else do the work and the worrying for me."

With a chuckle, she added, "Sorry, Haylie, but it's true. You've been a lifesaver."

Haylie offered the bride-to-be a genuine smile. "My pleasure. That's what I'm here for, after all."

Well, that and determining Bradley's paternity, but sometimes the less said in front of two dozen witnesses, the better.

"Do you think…" Avery paused, biting her lower lip nervously. "Maybe after Erica and Christian's big day, and you've had a chance to take a bit of a breather, could we sit down and chat? You've done so much for them on short notice, if you're not too worn out by then, maybe we could discuss another small, private ceremony for just after the New Year."

Avery looked to her fiancé for his opinion on the matter, and Guy nodded in agreement. Haylie had a feeling Avery could suggest a speedy elopement and he would have them halfway to Las Vegas before she finished her sentence.

"We won't rain on your parade, though," Avery added, leaning forward to glance down the full length of the table at Melissa and Shane, who were also expecting and scheduled to tie the knot on New Year's Eve.

Haylie wasn't even sure she would be around after the New Year, but since she'd gotten involved in Erica's wedding mainly to build her portfolio and hopefully garner even more wealthy clients in the future, it seemed silly not to agree to Avery's request.

Besides, Haylie was enjoying working with the staff at Jarrod Ridge, and would be happy to do so for a second event. She would even help Trevor's sister Melissa with her upcoming wedding, if she needed any assistance, but Haylie suspected the plans were pretty well ironed out by now.

"I'd love to," Haylie said. Then, belatedly realizing she probably should have checked with Trevor before offering her services to yet another member of his immediate family, she added, "If that's all right with you."

After all, regardless of what they shared in the wee hours of night, in the privacy of his bedroom, he might not want her around once the DNA tests came back and he knew whether or not he was Bradley's father.

If he was, he might even want her gone—as in, *give me my child and never darken my doorstep again.* And if he wasn't…well, he might feel the same either way.

But his response was quick enough and sure enough that she thought he must be sincere.

"Of course," Trevor murmured a moment before swinging his attention to his brother and soon-to-be sister-in-law. "Just be sure you're not stingy when it comes to her fee. I've been telling her all month how generous we Jarrods are, and I'd hate to have you ruin our reputation in her eyes by getting married on the cheap."

The statement was made in a jesting tone, but she suspected there was a note of seriousness underscoring the words as well. She didn't know whether to be flattered that he was watching out for her…or embarrassed by the attention he was drawing. To her, to him—to them.

"If she makes my Avery happy and does as impressive a job for us as she has for those two," Guy said, tipping his head in Christian and Erica's direction, "she can have a blank check. Hell, she can have the whole checkbook."

Trevor nodded in approval at his brother's quick, magnanimous response. Leaning toward Haylie, he murmured, "See, I told you we'd make it worth your while to stick around."

Then he winked and squeezed her knee under the table, making her feel as though a neon sign was hanging over her head flashing the words *Sleeping with Trevor Jarrod* for the whole world to see. Surely everyone in the room must be thinking that very thing about her.

But before she could burst into flames of mortification, to Haylie's immense relief, conversation picked up and moved in an entirely different direction. The main course was served, followed by a truly decadent chocolate-caramel-mocha dessert created by Guy himself, and then coffee.

Before she knew it—possibly because she was used to staying behind the scenes rather than being smack in the middle of them—Erica and Christian were standing, thanking everyone for coming and for being a part of their very special day, and then the guests began to leave.

Trevor collected their coats and waited patiently while she ran around making sure everything was cleared away properly and that nothing was left undone. She'd told him he could go home without her, or down to his office to catch up on some of the work she knew he'd fallen behind on ever since she'd shown up and thrown his life into turmoil. But he'd refused, telling her not to be silly, and then promptly seated himself at the bar to finish the glass of scotch he'd nursed all through dinner.

When she was finally ready, they made their way out of the lounge and through the hotel to the rear parking lot. Some resort guests were still milling about, but it was late enough that the halls were less busy and crowded than usual.

To Haylie's surprise, as they neared the exit, Trevor took her hand, holding it tightly all the way to his car. His touch warmed her. Not only her bare, chilled fingers, but his heat seeped through her skin to her bones, chasing the cold away, from the tips of her toes to the top of her head.

He must have been confident, though, that no one would see them, otherwise she knew he wouldn't have risked such an intimate gesture.

She didn't want to consider too closely how it made her feel, either. Mostly because she was very afraid she would feel *too much*.

As often as she told herself their involvement was *just* a convenient affair, just a fun way to pass a few hours during her stay in Aspen, lately that reasoning had become more and more difficult to believe.

Trevor was a great guy. Handsome, smart, successful. Rich, partly due to the family he came from, but also in his own right because of the business he'd built from the ground up. He was thoughtful and kind, wonderful with the baby....

If she did an internet search for "The Perfect Man," she was pretty sure his picture would pop right up. If she were filling out a questionnaire for one of those matchmaking services, everything she was looking for in a Mr. Right would describe him to a T.

Yet, ironically, he was the one man in the known universe she needed to be most wary of. The one she should have been smart enough to stay away from.

Coming to Aspen to confront him probably hadn't been the brightest idea to begin with. Letting him talk her into sticking around to await paternity results had been only slightly less intelligent. But going to bed with him...*continuing* to sleep with him even though she knew better, was downright dangerous.

So she couldn't be falling in love with him. It didn't matter that her heart flipped over in her chest the minute he walked in a room. Or that her insides turned all warm and mushy at the first hint of his cologne.

It didn't matter that she found herself wanting to spend more and more time with him, even if it was only to share a meal or kick back and watch a bit of television. Or that making love with him was the single most amazing experience of her life—over and over and over again. And it just seemed to get better every time they were together.

No, none of that mattered, because falling in love with him would not only be foolish...it was pointless.

Even if she was beginning to develop questionable feelings for Trevor...and she wasn't, not really...she had no doubt he was still completely feeling free. He was enjoying their time together—and what red-blooded American man suddenly presented with the luxury of a no-strings live-in lover wouldn't? But she was sure that for him, it didn't go beyond sex. Sex, and finding out if he was Bradley's father; that was the extent of his involvement.

Which was fine with her. She would be going back to Denver soon, anyway, so she needed to keep the very same mind-set.

Of course, reminding herself that she and Trevor were sharing "just good sex" didn't stop her from looking forward to it. As he pulled slowly up his drive and into the garage, she wondered if Bradley would be asleep already, and how quickly they could get rid of the sitter

Trevor had arranged to have watch the baby while they were at Erica's rehearsal dinner.

They exited the Hummer, and he took her arm as they climbed the porch steps and opened the front door. The babysitter—a college student who worked as a part-time server at one of the Ridge restaurants, was on the sofa. Her bare feet were propped on the coffee table, Bradley cradled in her lap, gumming the long, floppy ear of a stuffed bunny.

After shrugging out of their coats, Haylie took Bradley while Trevor paid the girl and saw her safely to her car.

"I'm going to take Bradley upstairs," Haylie told Trevor when he returned. "See if I can get him to sleep."

Trevor nodded. "I'll be up in a few minutes."

Standing at the landing, he watched Haylie climb the stairs. It was too attractive a sight to miss.

Once she disappeared around the corner, he loosened his tie and turned toward his office—or what used to be his office, at any rate. At his urging, Haylie had turned the spacious den into Wedding Central, but he was still allowed to enter as long as he promised not to touch anything.

Surprisingly, that particular order had come from his sister rather than Haylie. As comfortable as she'd become with living in his house, Haylie still acted like a guest instead of a live-in…whatever she was, exactly. But Trevor couldn't seem to break her of the habit of asking if she could use his fax machine or spread her paperwork out on the kitchen island. And that bothered him, more than he would have expected.

Erica, however, possessed no such qualms. And God help anyone who misplaced a sample menu or put so much as a finger on the ten-thousand-dollar designer gown Haylie had picked up for her earlier that week.

Careful not to disturb anything, he took a seat behind the desk and turned on the computer. While he waited for the system to boot so he could check his personal email, he picked up the phone and checked for voice-mail messages.

There was only one, but hearing Dr. Lazlo identify himself had Trevor's heart and stomach plummeting. He didn't even know what the doctor's message was going to be yet, and already his muscles were tensing, his chest growing tight with a mix of anticipation and dread.

"Mr. Jarrod, this is Dr. Lazlo," the other man's voice intoned. "I realize it's late, but the results of your tests have come in, and I know you're eager to hear them. I'll be in the office for a while yet, and after that, you can reach me on my cell phone. I'll be at your disposal all weekend, in case you don't get this message right away." He recited both numbers, and Trevor quickly jotted them down.

Heart still pounding in his chest, Trevor disconnected, then began to dial. This was it—the moment of truth. In the next couple of minutes, he would know one way or the other whether Bradley was his son.

A few weeks ago, he had known exactly which side of the fence he hoped the results would fall. *No match. Ninety-nine percent chance this is not your child.*

But that was before Haylie and Bradley had moved in with him. Before he'd learned how to change a diaper and mix formula and give a baby a bath. All things he never could have imagined he'd enjoy…but realized now he did.

He looked forward to them, even. Looked forward to

waking up in the morning and seeing Bradley's bright eyes and adorably pudgy baby cheeks. Looked forward to holding him while he drank a bottle or dodging splatters of carrot puree while he attempted to feed him his lunch.

And then there was Haylie. He *really* hadn't anticipated becoming attached to her, but damned if he didn't look forward to seeing her first thing each morning, too. Preferably right beside him in his bed, naked and drowsily welcoming.

Not only was she beautiful and headstrong, but she had no trouble standing up to him, which was in itself an unusual and admirable trait. He also admired how hard she'd worked to give Erica a perfect wedding day, with all that entailed. Add to that the incredible love and care she showed for Bradley, and it was possible she was as close to being the ideal woman as one could get.

Not something Trevor ever would have thought he'd catch himself considering. He was much more familiar with women of the flashy-but-flawed variety. And that had been fine, because he was never with any of them for very long.

But Haylie was different, and had him thinking outside the "temporary amusement" box.

Before he could contemplate *that* notion too closely, the doctor picked up the other end of the line.

"Dr. Lazlo, it's Trevor Jarrod," he identified himself. He didn't have to say anything more; they both knew why he was calling.

A minute later, he thanked the doctor for his time, then returned the phone to its cradle and sat back in his chair, letting the breath he'd been holding for what seemed like forever slide slowly from his lungs.

"Hey," Haylie said from the doorway. "Is everything all right?"

He lifted his head to look at her, saying nothing for a moment as he took in her long blond hair, bow-shaped mouth and gently rounded curves. Then he pushed himself up and moved across the crowded office space.

"I have some news," he said softly.

She tipped her head to the side. "Good news, I hope."

"I think so," he replied honestly. "The doctor called while we were away. The paternity results came in, and I *am* Bradley's father."

He wasn't sure what he'd expected—cheers or a cocky *I told you so,* maybe? Instead, a look of near panic passed over Haylie's features, quickly tamped down and replaced by stoic indifference.

"That's great. Wonderful. I'm happy for you."

The high pitch and speed of the words belied her sincerity, and for some reason that bothered the hell out of him. Hadn't she been the one to show up in his office without warning, bluntly informing him that he was the father of her sister's child? She should be delighted to have been proved right, rubbing his nose in it, even.

But as quickly as annoyance flashed, it was gone as he realized how she must be feeling. Yes, she'd been proven right in her belief that he was Bradley's father, but where did that leave her? Was he going to fight for full custody? Would he take the baby and cut her out of her nephew's life forever?

He wasn't sure yet about the first, but to the second, the answer was a big, fat, unequivocal *NO!* He wouldn't do that to Haylie *or* to Bradley. And out of the blue, he knew exactly what needed to be done.

"So now that we're sure, I think I know what our next step should be."

He watched her lips thin and her cheeks pale. But he didn't want to make her nervous, didn't want horrible, frightening scenarios running through her head when he could bring an immediate end to her unwarranted anxieties.

"I think we should get married."

Thirteen

Haylie felt like a Ping-Pong ball, being paddled from one end of a table to the other and back again. She'd gone from wanting to get the baby to sleep so she could come back downstairs and work at seducing Trevor into bed, to being panicked that there was no question about his paternity any longer and that he might try for full custody, to having the rug yanked out from under her with a shocking and unexpected proposal.

For a long, oxygen-deprived minute, all she could do was stand there, staring at Trevor. Blinking stupidly while her brain struggled to make sense of the sudden awkward tilt to her world.

"I—I—" Her mouth was open, but only stammered, stumbling sounds came out.

"It makes sense," Trevor supplied, looking about as moved and romantic as a wet sponge. "You're Bradley's legal guardian. We now know that Bradley is my biological child. And I think it's become clear over the past week that we're more than compatible physically."

He reached out to grasp her wrist, letting the pad of his thumb play over the inside pulse, as a hint of a smile played at one corner of his mouth.

"Getting married seems like the perfect solution to all of our problems. It will alleviate any concerns about custody, keep the press from turning into a pack of rabid wolves the minute they catch wind that I fathered a child with a complete stranger, and give Bradley what he needs most—a loving father *and* mother."

Haylie swallowed hard, trying to get a hold on her runaway emotions and put some kind of order to her scrambled thoughts.

On the one hand, she was happy they finally had their answer, that they—Trevor, especially—knew without a doubt that Bradley was his son. She hadn't been lying, hadn't come to him with some crazy, made-up story and dollar signs dancing in her head.

On the other hand, this news put a giant, ragged hole in the little bubble she'd allowed herself to live in these past few weeks. The one that let her believe everything was fine, that let her enjoy her time with Trevor, being under his roof, pretending that the fictitious happily-ever-after fantasy she'd invented would last forever.

But she'd always known it wouldn't, she just hadn't expected it to end quite this abruptly or in quite this way.

And she certainly hadn't expected Trevor to propose marriage.

Great sex was *not* a good enough reason to get married. Neither was primary physical custody of a child they both loved and wanted desperately. The fact that he was suggesting they tie the knot in such a cold, calculated manner told her that much.

He made it sound like a business proposition. A deal that would benefit them both.

And maybe it would. On paper, it all sounded very logical.

They both wanted Bradley, and by marrying, they could both keep him.

She worked well with his sisters, and had proven she could plan grand parties and events at Jarrod Ridge, as well as anywhere else in Aspen, Denver or beyond.

They suited each other well in bed, so even if their marriage was a loveless one, there would be no lack of passion.

But that was the problem, wasn't it? Any union between them would be completely lacking in what it needed most—*love*.

Worse, she was very much afraid that would only be true from his point of view, because she'd already fallen a little bit in love with him, hadn't she? It didn't seem possible, given that they'd only known each other for three weeks, but it was true, all the same.

She didn't think she could agree to a business arrangement marriage with him, and then go through the rest of her life loving him even though she knew he would never love her in return. And if he went back to his old habits of being a smooth, suave ladies' man, sleeping with other women on the side... *That* would surely kill her.

"I—I—" She caught herself stammering again and made herself stop, take a deep breath and start over.

"No," she said more firmly. With conviction. "No, I don't think that would be a very good idea at all. I don't need a marriage certificate to provide for Bradley—or your money. I'm perfectly capable of caring for him on my own, back in Denver, just as I have since the day he was born. You can see him, of course. Anytime. I won't ever try to keep you from him, and I'm sure we can work out a reasonable visitation schedule. But I'm not going to marry you simply because you think it would be an amusing convenience."

For a minute, Haylie didn't think he was going to respond, but she knew from the narrowing of his eyes and tightening of his mouth that he wasn't happy with her answer. Then he released her wrist and crossed his arms in front of his chest, regarding her with cold, dark eyes.

"I'm afraid that's unacceptable," he told her in no uncertain terms. "A child should know *both* of his parents. I'm Bradley's father, and for all intents and purposes, you're his mother. I don't want him shuffled back and forth between the two of us like a piece of luggage. After only recently discovering I have a half sister, and just now getting to know my own son, there's no way I'm going to let him out of my sight again."

"And that's the only reason you want to get married?" she asked quietly.

She didn't mean to, but she found herself holding her breath, waiting for his reply. Maybe he did have feelings for her. Even if it wasn't head-over-heels, undying love, maybe there was *something* there. Something they could build on, that would give her hope for the future.

"Of course," he answered. "Marriage is the best plan of action I can think of that will give us both what we want."

So much for rose petals and arias and heartfelt declarations of love.

"I'm sorry," she said, shaking her head and feeling the sadness of the words all the way to her soul. "I can't."

She felt Trevor's emotional withdrawal even before he stepped back, distancing himself physically.

"I'm sorry, too," he told her in a hard, flat voice. "And I'd urge you to reconsider. If you push me on this, I'm afraid I'll have to play hardball. I'll file for custody, Haylie, and you know that as Bradley's biological father, the courts will give him to me."

Not to mention his power and money and influence. He was right; if it came down to a court battle over Bradley, she would lose every time.

Careful not to touch her in any way, he moved around her and out of the office, leaving her alone to reflect upon his less than veiled threat.

For the first time since Haylie had started sharing his bed, Trevor woke up alone. He was sure it was only his imagination that led him to believe the room was quieter, the sheets cooler and less welcoming than when she was there.

With any luck, though, it wouldn't last.

They'd both gone to bed angry last night. After being turned down flat by the only woman he'd ever proposed marriage to, he'd let his temper get the better of him and stormed off to nurse his bruised ego.

He was sure Haylie hadn't felt much like singing after he'd left her in the den, either. He shouldn't have threatened her, and saying he would file for custody in order to take Bradley from her had been just that.

Surely there was a compromise to be made, some middle ground where they could agree on what was best for Bradley and how their relationship should proceed. He still thought marriage was the smartest way to go.

And there were worse situations he could think of than having Haylie in his bed every night and every morning, of sharing his home with her, of raising Bradley with her.

The more he thought about it, the more he liked the idea, and decided to bring it up to her one more time. Maybe in the bright light of day, she would be more agreeable to seeing sense.

After grabbing a quick shower, he dressed for work, then went downstairs, expecting to find Haylie there, fussing with Bradley and getting ready to go with him to the Ridge. Instead, he found the first level eerily quiet, the kitchen empty and exactly as they'd left it last evening.

With a frown beginning to mar his brow, he checked the other rooms just to be sure she wasn't tucked away somewhere, working on more wedding plans. When he didn't find Haylie or the baby, he climbed back upstairs, stopping in front of her bedroom door. Her *closed* bedroom door, which she normally left open during the day when she or the baby weren't in there.

Tapping gently, he waited for a reply. When he didn't get one, he tapped again and called her name. Nothing.

Trying the handle, he found the door unlocked and slowly pushed it open…only to find the room just as empty as the rest of the house. The bed was made, the baby's things missing from the crib and changing table, Haylie's belongings gone from the closet and bathroom vanity.

A slick feeling of dread began to trickle down his spine, tightening his chest and gut. If their things were gone, then that meant …

Taking the steps two at a time, he hurried back

downstairs to search again. Everything. Every room, every broom closet, and finally the garage. The Escalade was still there, but her older, less roadworthy hunk of junk was not. It was gone, and so, he feared, were Haylie and Bradley.

She'd left him. Packed up in the middle of the night and taken off. Back to Denver, no doubt. Without a word. Without even leaving a note.

Dammit. He didn't know who he was more upset with: Haylie for running away—with his son, no less—or himself for royally messing up last night's difference of opinion.

Not quite sure what to do or how to handle the situation, he climbed behind the wheel of his Hummer and headed for Jarrod Ridge. He would go to the office, just as he'd planned. Work out his anger and frustrations at the computer, and maybe later on the slopes.

He certainly wasn't going to go racing off to Denver, chasing after her like a lovesick fool. At least not until he knew what his next plan of action—with Haylie, with Bradley, with both of them—should be.

Hours later, Trevor had several tabs open on his computer screen, several files spread across his desk... and didn't feel as though he'd gotten a damn thing done since he'd walked in the office.

A rap on the door caught his attention and increased his level of annoyance, which had been steadily growing as the day progressed.

"What?" he snapped, not bothering to look up from what he was doing. Part of the convenience of working weekends was fewer interruptions. In theory.

When he raised his head, he found himself staring into the eyes of his older brother Blake.

Looking tall and commanding, as usual, Blake wore his role as leader of the Jarrod family and Jarrod Ridge as well as he wore his tailored, gray Armani suit. He also looked as though he knew Trevor was out of sorts and wondering at the cause.

Not waiting for an invitation, his brother strode forward and took a seat opposite Trevor's.

"Word has it you're in a lousy mood today and taking it out on your lovely and talented receptionist. Much more, and I'm afraid she might walk."

With a sigh, Trevor dropped his pen and rubbed his eyes. "I know. I'll send her flowers and increase her Christmas bonus by way of an apology."

"An actual apology might help, too," Blake suggested.

Trevor nodded. "Before I leave for the day."

"Good." His brother smoothed the crease in his slacks, obviously searching for his next words. "So what's the cause of this suddenly sour disposition? Care to share?" he asked.

Leaning back in his chair, Trevor rested his hands on his stomach and decided that his older brother might not be the worst person to confide in at the moment.

"Haylie's gone," Trevor admitted. Even voicing that fact hurt, let alone picturing his house as he'd last seen it—empty, empty, empty.

"Gone?" Blake repeated. "As in gone-gone?"

"As in packed up her belongings and the baby and went back to Denver," he bit out, every word stinging like a paper cut.

"Any reason why she'd just up and take off like that?"

Trevor took a deep breath, then slowly let it out. "Paternity results came back. Bradley is mine."

Blake's eyes flashed wide. "That's terrific." Then after a second, he said, "It is good news, isn't it?"

"Hell, yes," Trevor responded without a qualm. He might not have planned to become a parent at this point in his life, if ever, but now that Bradley was here, and he knew for certain that the boy was his son... Well, he was just about bursting with love and pride for the kid. And he missed him, dammit. Already.

"I take it Haylie doesn't feel the same," Blake said carefully. "Is she going to fight you for custody?"

"I don't know," Trevor replied honestly. "We didn't quite get that far."

"So why did she leave?"

That caused Trevor's lips to twist. "I guess she didn't feel comfortable living with me any longer after I asked her to marry me and she turned me down flat."

Blowing out a surprised breath, Blake sat back. "Wow. I have to tell you, that surprises me. The way you two have been getting along these past few weeks, I would have expected her to accept. Or at least stick around long enough to see where things between you could lead."

"Tell me about it," Trevor muttered.

"Never thought I'd see the day a woman turned you down for anything, little brother," Blake teased. "Especially once you told her you loved her."

Trevor's eyes widened. "Whoa," he said, rocking uncomfortably in his chair. "Who said anything about love?"

For a minute, dead silence echoed through the room. And then Blake said, "Please tell me you didn't propose without telling her you love her."

When Trevor didn't respond, Blake added in a tone

part disbelieving, part chastising, "What were you thinking?"

Sitting up straight, Trevor moved to rest his forearms on his desk. "It isn't about love," he told his brother, "it's about what's best for Bradley."

"And what would that be?"

"Having two loving parents in his life, full time. Not being passed back and forth between caretakers and residences like an afterthought."

If anyone should have been able to understand Trevor's feelings on the subject of caring for and raising Bradley, it was Blake, who had a child of his own on the way now. One he at least knew about and could prepare for, Trevor thought wryly.

"Agreed. One hundred percent," his brother agreed. "But that's not what you're talking about, are you? You're talking about using a marriage certificate so you can have a live-in nanny. One who will also warm your bed."

Trevor blinked in surprise. Where did Blake get off making such a crass remark? One that was completely off base, no less.

"Don't be ridiculous," he scoffed. "If I wanted a nanny, live-in or otherwise, I'd simply hire one."

"Then why marry Haylie?"

"Because she's Bradley's aunt and has raised him his whole life. She might as well be his mother, she loves him so much and has taken such good care of him."

"Right," Blake said slowly. "And you want to marry her because…"

Trevor's brow crinkled in a frown. "I just told you—"

"No," his brother corrected, "you told me you want to keep Haylie in Bradley's life, and having her move to

Aspen to live with you would make that more convenient for you. What you *haven't* told me is why you want to make her your wife. To have and to hold, in sickness and in health… I'm sure you've heard the vows before."

Growing aggravated with Blake's obscure riddles, Trevor sighed and rubbed the bridge of his nose where a headache was forming. "What's your point?" he asked.

"Given your dating history, I'd think you'd have picked up on this by now. But my *point,* little brother, is that no woman wants to be asked for her hand in marriage because you're interested in full-time child care. They want flowers and candy and romance. A diamond the size of a walnut wouldn't hurt, either, but you can't just say, 'Hey, I think we should get married so we can both live under the same roof and raise my son together.' Especially not to a successful, independent woman like Haylie."

Well, when he put it that way…

A sinking feeling filled Trevor's stomach at the knowledge that that's exactly how he'd proposed to Haylie. Blunt, straightforward, unemotional.

He realized, too, that he hadn't even *asked* her to marry him, but had simply told her that's what he thought they should do. He'd proposed business deals with more enthusiasm than he'd proposed marriage to a woman he honest-to-goodness cared for.

In his defense, though, this was all new to him. He'd never even considered asking a woman to marry him before. Never thought about what it would be like to spend the rest of his life with someone. "Love" was still off his radar and a bit too disconcerting to contemplate, but he was willing to admit he felt *something* for Haylie.

More than he'd feel for just a live-in nanny, thank you very much, he nearly blurted out to Blake. But since he'd apparently already made enough of an ass of himself where his brother was concerned, he decided to keep his mouth shut.

"Will you take a word of advice from your big brother?" Blake asked when Trevor remained oddly quiet.

"Sure." At this point, he'd take anything he could get.

"Figure out how you feel about her. *Really* feel about her. And if the idea of going through the rest of your life without her in it makes you want to crawl into a hole and die, don't waste another minute on the *whys* or *what-ifs*. Go to her and tell her how you feel. Use the L-word—repeatedly and with great enthusiasm. As someone else who let his pride get in the way of love for far too long, I'm here to tell you you'll never be sorry."

With that, Blake pushed to his feet, straightened his suit jacket and moved toward the door. Grasping the handle, he turned back and fixed Trevor with a sober glance.

"For the record," Blake said quietly, "we all really like Haylie. She's good for you. And personally, I think you'd be an idiot if you let her get away."

Without waiting for a response—not that Trevor had one to offer—Blake left the office, closing the door behind him.

So his brothers and sisters and their significant others all liked Haylie, and had obviously been speculating about their relationship behind his back. He should be annoyed, but surprisingly, he wasn't. He wanted the family to like her.

What he had to figure out, as Blake had suggested, was how *he* felt about her. And what he was going to do about it once he did.

Fourteen

Why was it that when she was in a hurry, everything including the kitchen sink seemed to fall in her path?

The last thing Haylie needed—because she *was* in a hurry—was another interruption eating up her time and throwing her even more off schedule. But that's exactly what she got with a knock on her door bright and early Monday morning.

Thanks to being up half the night with Bradley, who had decided to develop colic and been too cranky to sleep, she was already running dreadfully late. For her first day back at the office after her extended absence, too. Her employees were quite capable and reliable, but still she knew she would be walking into a beehive of activity and returning to a giant game of catch-up.

She wished now that she'd given herself more than just one short weekend of being back in Denver before once again jumping into the fray. She should have simply stayed home without letting anyone know she was actually back. A few days tucked into bed with a gallon of Rocky Road and a stack of tearjerker DVDs sounded better than jumping immediately back into the fray, that was for sure.

Not only that, but in addition to trying to juggle her return to It's Your Party, she would also be making the long trek back to Aspen tomorrow already…and probably several more times this week because Erica's wedding was on Friday. Because regardless of her feelings for Trevor at the moment—or the fact that she'd let herself develop feelings for him *at all*—she would never leave his sister in the lurch.

Admittedly, she'd picked up and taken off without warning and without thinking through every detail of her sudden disappearance. But as soon as she'd gotten home, she'd done the responsible thing by picking up the phone and calling Erica.

She hadn't mentioned Trevor's name at all, even though it hadn't been easy. But she'd been afraid that if she spoke about him, if she so much as *thought* about him while talking with his sister, she would burst into tears.

So she'd stuck to the facts, or the facts as she was making them up for Erica's benefit, telling her that she'd been called back to Denver on a business "emergency," but assuring her that she would return to Aspen as often as necessary, and that everything connected to her Christmas Eve wedding would go off without a hitch.

And she intended to follow through on her promise. She only hoped she would be able to navigate the ins and outs of Jarrod Ridge—especially the Manor—without running into Trevor.

It wouldn't be easy, that was for sure. She might even

have to hire a few extra assistants to run errands for her so that she could hole up in one of the back conference rooms or ballrooms where no one was likely to find her. And she would definitely need to ask someone to run to Trevor's house to collect all of her and Erica's things from his office.

With a groan, she once again bemoaned her hasty decision to pack up and leave rather than sticking around and simply dealing with the up-front knowledge that Trevor wanted her in his bed, wanted her as a caretaker for Bradley, but didn't want *her*. Not really.

The doorbell rang again, making her want to tear her hair out. She chose instead to mutter a strained curse beneath her breath. The baby was still fussy, she'd spilled formula on the first outfit she'd put on, she couldn't seem to find her keys, and now—*now*—someone was on her doorstep, beckoning her to become even more frazzled and late.

It had better be something important, like her landlord reporting a gas leak or a firefighter needing to rescue her from a five-alarm blaze. Because if it was just an annoying salesperson or a neighbor wanting to borrow a cup of sugar, she wouldn't be responsible for her actions.

With Bradley whimpering from his baby seat in the kitchen, she raced for the front of the apartment, searching for her keys as she went. Yanking the door open with every intention of blurting out, "I don't want any," no matter what the person standing on the other side was selling, she stopped short.

The first thing she saw was flowers—a gigantic bouquet of soft pink lilies and roses filling nearly the entire space of the open door. Then a gold-wrapped box the size of a small continent appeared. And higher, as her gaze traveled beyond the outlandish offerings, she found Trevor.

He was dressed in one of his elegant, tailored suits, face smooth and freshly shaven, his dark hair stylishly tousled. He looked like a million bucks—which was probably how much he'd spent on the flowers and what she assumed were gourmet chocolates. But it was Trevor himself, not the gifts, that made her mouth go dry and her head spin like a top.

Then she remembered their last interaction, and his threats to take Bradley from her by any means necessary. Grip tightening on the knob, she was ready to slam the door in his face, ready to grab the baby and jump out a rear window if she had to.

"What are you doing here?" she asked, keeping her voice carefully controlled, and trying not to let her anger or fear seep into her tone.

"I had a rough weekend after you left," he told her, not mincing words. His dark brown gaze was steady, the corners of his mouth drawn tight.

"Wandered around the house without answering the phone or checking my email. Didn't even hit the slopes or get any work done, which is what I usually do when I need to think. I also had a bit of a heart-to-heart with my brother Blake. Among other things, he pointed out that women don't get swept away by being told they should get married for practical reasons. They want flowers and candy and grand romantic gestures. So here I am, with the first two, at least."

He thrust the flowers and box of chocolates at her, catching her off guard enough that she released her hold on the door and took them, clutching them to her chest.

"As for the grand romantic gesture…"

Reaching into his pocket, he took out a small, heart-shaped box of black velvet—one that looked disturbingly like a ring box—and dropped to one knee.

Oh, my God. Was this really happening, or was she dreaming it? Haylie's eyes widened as the room began to spin around her, her brain struggling to process what she was seeing, to make sense, not only of Trevor's sudden appearance on her doorstep, but of his words and actions, as well.

"As much as I hate to admit it, Blake is kind of a smart guy. He also mentioned that if I just want someone to love and take care of Bradley, I can hire a nanny. But that if I cared for *you,* I needed to stop being such an idiot and tell you so."

Her heart was pounding so hard, it made a knocking sound inside her chest that echoed in her ears. Was this going where she thought it was? Maybe she wasn't hearing him correctly. Maybe he was here to tell her he'd hired that nanny to take care of Bradley and had only brought the candy and flowers in an attempt to soften the blow.

"That's where the restless weekend comes in. Once I sat down—or rather, paced a hole in the floor—and really thought about it, I realized my brother was right. I don't love only Bradley," he continued from his half-kneeling position. "And if the tests had shown he wasn't my son, I wouldn't have cared. I would still have wanted you to stick around. I figured it out, Haylie. The two nights of soul-searching worked."

She watched his Adam's apple do a slow drop and climb as he swallowed, feeling the same rush of nerves low in her own belly. Her heart *thu-thump thu-thump thu-thump*ed like a herd of wild horses in her chest, making it harder and harder for her to breathe.

"I love you. I love *you*, Haylie," he blurted out just before the rigidity in his perfectly squared shoulders eased a little.

"I've been with a lot of women," he admitted, "but I've never been in love. I guess that explains why I didn't recognize it when it finally happened to me. Why it took the sucker punch of you taking off in the middle of the night for me to wise up." His mouth curved up in one of her favorite wry, self-deprecating smiles.

"But here's what I do know. I know I've been happier and more content in the brief month I've known you than in all the rest of my adult life. I know the house is empty and lonely as hell without you and Bradley there to fill the space with warmth and laughter. And I know that when I think about never seeing you again, it feels as though someone is reaching into my chest cavity and ripping out not only my heart, but my soul."

Of their own volition, tears flooded her eyes. She didn't think she'd ever heard anything so beautiful, except maybe in her own head when she thought about him.

But did he mean it? Did he really and truly feel this way about her, or would he change his mind the minute some cute little twenty-four-year-old with a short skirt and surgically enhanced bosom crossed his path?

"So I'm here to propose again." He soldiered on. "This time, though, I'm going to *ask* instead of tell. And if you say yes, it won't be a marriage of convenience. I'll love you with every fiber of my being, and expect the same from you. I'll expect you to live with me, till death do us part, whether that means you relocating to Aspen or me moving here—I honestly don't care which."

Taking a deep breath, his voice softened only a fraction when he said, "And if you say no... Well, that's okay, too. I mean, I don't want you to say no, of course, but I'd understand. *Understanding* doesn't mean giving up, though. It just means I'll have to start from scratch and work twice as hard at convincing you that my feelings are genuine."

His eyes glittered with conviction as he added, "And no matter what, I won't try to take Bradley away from you. Ever. I don't want you to worry about that. I want him, don't get me wrong, but we'll work out a visitation schedule that we can both live with, I promise."

Popping the lid of the velvet box, he held it out to her, revealing a bright gold band and stunning, marquise-cut diamond that had to be three or four carats, at least. Every facet winked and sparkled, making her almost dizzy.

"Will you marry me, Haylie? Be my wife, my lover, the mother of my children—Bradley, as well as any more we decide to have together?"

Her chest was so tight, her lungs refused to function. Her heart, which had been racing at full speed only seconds before, seemed to screech to a halt.

She wanted so much to believe him, to throw herself into his arms and shout *yes, yes, yes!* Nothing would make her happier than to be with him. Forever. Even if it meant moving to Aspen, starting over in a whole new city, a whole new element. Or maybe not starting over, but branching out.

Could she? Should she?

Taking a shuddering breath, she looked deep into Trevor's eyes, and what she saw there warmed her more than any amount of flowers or candy or pretty words could. Love. And longing. And determination.

He loved her, he wanted her, and if she turned him down, he really would dig in his heels and fight for her.

For a moment, she considered saying no, just to see what he would do. Would there be more flowers, actual dates, attempts at wining and dining her in ways that only a millionaire Jarrod heir could?

But she didn't care about Trevor's money, did she? Or about being wooed. She only cared about him.

Letting go of the flowers and chocolates she'd been clutching to her chest, she fell to her knees in front of him and gave the only answer she could. The only one that made sense both in her head and in her heart.

"Yes," she whispered, throwing her arms around his neck and hugging him tight. His arms circled her waist, squeezing her just as tightly, and then his mouth covered hers, kissing away any further response.

For long minutes, they knelt there, simply kissing, holding, loving. When they finally came up for air, Trevor was grinning, and she could feel a damp smile of her own spreading across her face.

Wiping the tears from her cheeks with the pads of his thumbs, he kissed her one last time before producing the ring box and cocking his head to one side. "May I?"

"Please," she said, extending her left hand. Her *shaking* left hand.

He took it by the wrist and slid the diamond on her finger. As large as it was, she was surprised to find it didn't weigh more. But still, she couldn't resist lifting it up to the light, turning it this way and that, admiring the symbol of her love for Trevor, and his for her.

That he had picked it out just for her and come here to declare his feelings for her on bended knee... She would never forget this day, as long as she lived.

Climbing to his feet, Trevor pulled her up with him, still holding her close to his chest.

"I know we have a lot to discuss," he murmured, "and

you look like you were on your way out, but there are only two things I want right now—to say hello to my son, and then to put him down for a nap so I can make love to my beautiful fiancée."

His wolfish grin as he walked her backward into her apartment and kicked the door closed behind him made her chuckle.

"It's a little early for his nap, but he was up half the night, so you might get lucky." Kissing his ear, she whispered, "And just in case you do, I'd be happy to call in sick to work so you can get lucky with me, too."

Leaning back, he met her gaze, his expression serious. "I already have," he told her in a low voice. "I already have."

Epilogue

It was Christmas Eve.

Snow was falling softly outside the windows of one of the Manor's gorgeous ballrooms. Strands of tiny lights were strung along the walls and ceiling like a starry sky, and a humongous Douglas fir decorated with gold ribbons and ivory bulbs stood at the far end of the room.

Round tables draped in white linens spread out all around, leaving only the center dance floor bare, and guests mingled at both, dancing to a mix of romantic and holiday music played by a string quartet, or enjoying the last bites of wedding cake.

The guests of honor, the newly united Mr. and Mrs. Christian Hanford, were seated at a long, rectangular table reserved for the wedding party, but they had eyes only for each other. In fact, the longer the reception went on, the more they looked as though they couldn't wait to thank everyone for sharing in their special day, then take off for more enjoyable honeymoon pursuits.

Not that Haylie could blame them. She imagined that when her turn came to tie the knot, she would be just as eager to shed the formalities of the official event and get Trevor alone and out of his tuxedo.

A ripple of excitement ran beneath her skin, letting her know just how much she was anticipating her own wedding day. They'd barely discussed plans of any sort since he'd shown up at her door and proposed to her on bended knee, mostly because there were just too many other things going on at the moment.

She'd still needed to see to last-minute preparations for Erica and Christian's wedding. Then there was Melissa and Shane's New Year's Eve wedding, which she would be attending only as a guest, thank goodness. And immediately after, Avery and Guy's nuptials to contend with.

She still didn't know exactly when that would be taking place, but Avery had assured Haylie that she wanted her help with everything from setting a date to deciding on centerpieces.

Which was fine. Better than fine, actually, since one of the things she and Trevor *had* discussed was her carrying on her work here at the Ridge. Rather than closing down or relocating It's Your Party, they'd agreed that it would probably be smarter to leave the Denver business open and put one of her senior employees in charge.

Trevor had suggested that she then branch out and turn the company into a bit of a franchise, opening a second location—at the Ridge itself, if she preferred. He'd promised to help her find the perfect site on the premises to set up shop, but also wanted her to take over as the resort's event coordinator. It would mean getting involved in more than just weddings—it would mean anniversaries, birthdays, engagements, bachelorette parties, and she would certainly be available for any family celebrations.

She liked that idea. She liked the idea of working at the Ridge, being able to keep Bradley with her much of the time or leave him with very reliable day care when she couldn't, and of being able to walk down the hall or across the street whenever she felt compelled to see her soon-to-be husband. Maybe distract him from his computer screen or latest marketing plans.

When a pair of strong male hands slid around her waist and pulled her back against an equally strong male chest, she grinned, thinking that someone else's thoughts must have been running along the same lines as her own.

"You know," Trevor whispered in her ear, "I may have to change my mind about you becoming the event coordinator for Jarrod Ridge."

She jerked her head back, shocked and hurt.

"You're a little too good at this, and I'm afraid you'll be in such high demand once people figure that out that I'll never get to have you all to myself."

As the rest of his words sank in, she released a relieved breath, the cold chill of his perceived criticism replaced by a pleasurable warmth.

Of all the weddings she'd taken part in, she thought she was probably most proud of this one. Not only because she'd pulled it all together in such a short amount of time—and no matter how "simple" Erica had assured her she wanted her special day to be, there wasn't really anything simple about a wedding unless the couple eloped to Las Vegas. And even that involved booking airline tickets and finding a chapel.

But in addition to the food and decor, and keeping everything and everyone on schedule, the entire immediate Jarrod family was in attendance this evening. All the brothers and sisters, husbands and wives. And most surprising of all, Erica's father and stepmother were not only there to help celebrate their daughter's big day, but seemed to be getting along well with all of the Jarrods.

During their time together, Erica had told her about the shock and hurt of discovering that Walter Prentice, the man who'd raised her from birth, wasn't her biological father and that Donald Jarrod was. A fact she hadn't become aware of until after Donald's death. Given that the Prentices and Jarrods apparently hadn't gotten along all that well to begin with, it had taken all these months for the two families to overcome their differences.

Haylie was glad. Erica deserved to enjoy her wedding day without the stress of worrying about how the people she loved most in the world were going to act once they were in the same room together.

Turning her attention back to the man who was holding her snuggly against his chest, swaying back and forth to the airy notes of Chopin, Haylie said, "I was just thinking about that myself. Mostly about how convenient it would be to work here, knowing we could drop in on each other throughout the day."

"And why would we want to do that?" he murmured, feigning puzzlement even as his tone rang with amusement.

"Oh, I don't know. In case we need to discuss some pressing matter where Bradley is concerned. Or for the occasional office quickie. I've always had a fantasy about making love on a desk in the middle of the workday."

Her head spun as he whipped her around to face him. The tea-length skirt of her emerald-green gown swirled around her legs before rustling to a stop.

"You never told me that," Trevor ground out, his coffee-brown eyes narrowed and intense, one brow raised in keen interest.

She cocked her head to the side. "It's never come up before now. And you never asked," she replied primly.

His other brow went up in what she could only perceive as a challenging expression. "I've got a desk. Downstairs. And that's one fantasy I'd be happy to realize right now."

"But how would that look," she began, reaching up to straighten his already perfectly straight black tie, "for the wedding planner to go missing in the middle of the wedding reception? And you're the bride's brother. Your disappearance would look even worse."

Sliding a hand to the small of her back, he tugged her close, letting her feel the proof of his interest.

"You're assuming I care what anyone thinks. Let me assure you, I don't."

"I know you don't," she murmured softly.

That poise and self-confidence was one of the reasons she loved him. And it was going to come in handy once the media found out he was marrying her, the aunt of his nearly five-month-old illegitimate son.

She couldn't *wait* until that hit the fan. But as Trevor said and had assured her numerous times before, it didn't matter what others thought or how many crazy headlines the national tabloids invented. Only the truth mattered, and the truth was that she loved him to distraction, just as he loved her.

They had each other and Bradley, and maybe one day more children to add to their happy family. As far as Haylie was concerned, that made her life just about perfect.

"An hour," she told him, leaning her face into his. "One more hour, and whether the bride and groom have left or not, I'll let you whisk me down to your office and seduce me on top of your desk."

To her delight, Trevor responded with a low growl. The sound made her shiver, and she couldn't help but laugh.

"Sixty minutes," he agreed, synchronizing his watch, "and not a second more."

She nodded.

"In the meantime, how about a dance?"

Taking slow steps backward, he pulled her with him, and she went willingly, following him onto the dance floor and into the rest of her wonderful, happy-ever-after life.

* * * * *

COMING NEXT MONTH

Available January 11, 2011

#2059 HAVE BABY, NEED BILLIONAIRE
Maureen Child
Billionaires and Babies

#2060 CLAIMED: THE PREGNANT HEIRESS
Day Leclaire
The Takeover

#2061 HIS THIRTY-DAY FIANCÉE
Catherine Mann
Rich, Rugged & Royal

#2062 THE CEO'S ACCIDENTAL BRIDE
Barbara Dunlop

#2063 AMNESIAC EX, UNFORGETTABLE VOWS
Robyn Grady

#2064 PAPER MARRIAGE PROPOSITION
Red Garnier

SDCNM1210

REQUEST YOUR FREE BOOKS!

**2 FREE NOVELS
PLUS 2
FREE GIFTS!**

Silhouette® *Desire*®

Passionate, Powerful, Provocative!

YES! Please send me 2 FREE Silhouette Desire® novels and my 2 FREE gifts (gifts are worth about $10). After receiving them, if I don't wish to receive any more books, I can return the shipping statement marked "cancel." If I don't cancel, I will receive 6 brand-new novels every month and be billed just $4.05 per book in the U.S. or $4.74 per book in Canada. That's a saving of at least 15% off the cover price! It's quite a bargain! Shipping and handling is just 50¢ per book.* I understand that accepting the 2 free books and gifts places me under no obligation to buy anything. I can always return a shipment and cancel at any time. Even if I never buy another book, the two free books and gifts are mine to keep forever.

225/326 SDN E5QG

Name _____ (PLEASE PRINT)

Address _____ Apt. #

City _____ State/Prov. _____ Zip/Postal Code

Signature (if under 18, a parent or guardian must sign)

Mail to the Silhouette Reader Service:

IN U.S.A.: P.O. Box 1867, Buffalo, NY 14240-1867
IN CANADA: P.O. Box 609, Fort Erie, Ontario L2A 5X3

Not valid for current subscribers to Silhouette Desire books.

**Want to try two free books from another line?
Call 1-800-873-8635 or visit www.morefreebooks.com.**

* Terms and prices subject to change without notice. Prices do not include applicable taxes. N.Y. residents add applicable sales tax. Canadian residents will be charged applicable provincial taxes and GST. Offer not valid in Quebec. This offer is limited to one order per household. All orders subject to approval. Credit or debit balances in a customer's account(s) may be offset by any other outstanding balance owed by or to the customer. Please allow 4 to 6 weeks for delivery. Offer available while quantities last.

Your Privacy: Silhouette Books is committed to protecting your privacy. Our Privacy Policy is available online at www.eHarlequin.com or upon request from the Reader Service. From time to time we make our lists of customers available to reputable third parties who may have a product or service of interest to you. If you would prefer we not share your name and address, please check here. ☐

Help us get it right—We strive for accurate, respectful and relevant communications. To clarify or modify your communication preferences, visit us at www.ReaderService.com/consumerchoice.

SDES10R

HARLEQUIN®

A *Romance*

FOR EVERY MOOD™

Spotlight on

Classic

Quintessential, modern love stories
that are romance at its finest.

**See the next page
to enjoy a sneak peek from
the Harlequin Presents® series.**

*Harlequin Presents® is thrilled
to introduce the first installment of
an epic tale of passion and drama by*
USA TODAY *Bestselling Author*
Penny Jordan!

**When buttoned-up Giselle first meets
the devastatingly handsome Saul Parenti,
the heat between them is explosive....**

"LET ME GET THIS STRAIGHT. Are you actually suggesting
that I would stoop to that kind of game playing?"

Saul came out from behind his desk and walked toward
her. Giselle could smell his hot male scent and it was making
her dizzy, igniting a low, dull, pulsing ache that was taking
over her whole body.

Giselle defended her suspicions. "You don't want me here."

"No," Saul agreed, "I don't."

And then he did what he had sworn he would not do,
cursing himself beneath his breath as he reached for her,
pulling her fiercely into his arms and kissing her with all
the pent-up fury she had aroused in him from the moment
he had first seen her.

Giselle certainly *wanted* to resist him. But the hand she
raised to push him away developed a will of its own and
was sliding along his bare arm beneath the sleeve of his
shirt, and the body that should have been arching away
from him was instead melting into him.

Beneath the pressure of his kiss he could feel and taste
her gasp of undeniable response to him. He wanted to
devour her, take her and drive them both until they were
equally satiated—even whilst the anger within him that
she should make him feel that way roared and burned its

resentment of his need.

She was helpless, Giselle recognized, totally unable to withstand the storm lashing at her, able only to cling to the man who was the cause of it and pray that she would survive.

Somewhere else in the building a door banged. The sound exploded into the sensual tension that had enclosed them, driving them apart. Saul's chest was rising and falling as he fought for control; Giselle's whole body was trembling.

Without a word she turned and ran.

Find out what happens when Saul and Giselle succumb to their irresistible desire in

THE RELUCTANT SURRENDER

Available January 2011 from Harlequin Presents®

Silhouette Desire

HAVE BABY,
NEED BILLIONAIRE

MAUREEN CHILD

Simon Bradley is accomplished, successful
and very proud. The fact that he has to
prove he's fit to be a father to his own child
is preposterous. Especially when he has to
prove it to Tula Barrons, one of the most
scatterbrained women he's ever met. But Simon
has a ruthless plan to win Tula over and when
passion overrules prudence one night, it opens
up the door to an affair that leaves them both
staggering. Will this billionaire bachelor learn
to love more than his fortune?

Billionaires and Babies

Available January
wherever books are sold.

Always Powerful, Passionate and Provocative.